Praise for the Autho

'Lucid prose, wide knowledge and an impish sense of humour made him an instant hit with generations of Tamil readers'

Hindustan Times

'Sujatha continues to be extremely popular'

The Hindu

'A pioneer'

Times of India

'Sujatha did not consider writing as work, it was an act of love'

Kamal Hassan

A MYSTERY SET TO MUSIC

A MYSTERY SET TO MUSIC

SUJATHA

Translated by

MALINI SESHADRI

BLOOMSBURY

NEW DELHI • LONDON • OXFORD • NEW YORK • SYDNEY

BLOOMSBURY INDIA
Bloomsbury Publishing India Pvt. Ltd
Second Floor, LSC Building No. 4, DDA Complex, Pocket C – 6 & 7,
Vasant Kunj, New Delhi, 110070

BLOOMSBURY, BLOOMSBURY INDIA and the Diana logo
are trademarks of Bloomsbury Publishing Plc

Originally published in Tamil as *Karaiellam Shebagapoo*
by Poompuhar Publications in April 1979

First published in India 2024
This edition published 2024

ISBN: PB: 978-93-61316-89-0; eBook: 978-93-61312-74-8
2 4 6 8 10 9 7 5 3 1

Typeset in Fournier MT Std by Manipal Technologies Limited
Printed and bound in India by Thomson Press India Ltd

FSC www.fsc.org MIX Paper | Supporting responsible forestry FSC® C010615

A MYSTERY SET TO MUSIC

1

'Fields full of jasmine
Champaka flowers on the water's edge
See how the aroma pervades the whole land
Along the path taken by the righteous son.'
—Translated from a collection of Tamil folk songs by
N. Vanamamalai

THE PASSENGER TRAIN CHUGGED in slowly and came to a stop at the station platform as if it was affectionately indulging its passengers.

A young woman scurried around selling tender cucumbers. From the First Class carriage, a single passenger emerged—a young man carrying a blue suitcase and a guitar. A camera hung from a strap around his neck. In that setting, he appeared odd and alien. He looked around through his dark, shaded sunglasses.

It was a small station. Just one small room; on the far wall, in a niche, stood an ancient telephone. The stationmaster was busy speaking into it. The levers that operated the signals were set on the platform itself. A piece of broken railing dangled from the branch of a laburnum tree, apparently serving as a bell. A blue-shirted man came by and clanged on the 'bell' a couple of times, dislodging a few laburnum flowers from the tree in the process. Then, keys dangling from one hand, he walked towards the engine, eyeing the lone passenger all the while as if he had spotted a strange creature.

A single granite structure; at a little distance, just three houses. A dirt road snaked away from the station, apparently heading nowhere. A banyan tree stood adjacent to the station, draping its dangling roots around it as though to declare, 'This station belongs to me!'

The engine spoke briefly, spat a bit of its water load in a puff of steam, and started chugging away. The young cucumber-seller ran alongside on the platform. The passenger who had not paid her sat enjoying the sight of the young woman running, her breasts bouncing. He leaned out and casually tossed a few coins onto the platform. She stooped to pick up the coins and yelled a curse at him.

The blue-shirted railwayman approached the passenger. 'So you have got off here?' Again came the sound of a train in the distance.

'Yes, I need to go to Mempatti,' said the passenger, whose name was S.V. Kalyanaraman. 'How far is it from here?'

'It could be ... maybe ... five miles or so. Why are you going there?'

'I have some work there.'

'What? In Mempatti?'

'Yes. Is there a bus I can take?'

'A bus?' Blue Shirt laughed. He turned and called out to the young woman on the platform, 'Hey, cucumber, this man wants to go to your town.'

She was still grumbling about the crude passenger. 'That nasty fellow has cheated me of five annas! May the goddess Mariamman punish him.' She turned towards the passenger and saluted him smartly. 'Good morning, saar. Will you take a photo of me?'

The young woman's salute took the passenger by surprise. She seemed to be about eighteen, and with a good wash, could perhaps be pretty. On her dark face shone a red-stone nose ornament and a pair of ear studs. She was clad in a checked *sungadi* sari and a pink peppermint-candy-coloured blouse. A string of plastic beads adorned her neck, and her teeth were perfectly white. She appeared toned and fit, a sign of her hardworking, energetic lifestyle. With the added advantage of her youth, she was like a joyful raga. Kalyanaraman was reminded of Beethoven's symphony. In D Major, Opus 61.

'Come in, come in,' invited the stationmaster. Kalyanaraman stepped into the room. The stationmaster was in a dhoti teamed with a white coat, the latter merely a nod to convention. His lunch was ready on the table, with a fresh plantain leaf laid out. A bright green rolled-up signalling flag lay next to it.

'Did you arrive on the three nought one?'

'Why? Is there some other train too?'

'He wants to go to Mempatti,' said Blue Shirt.

'Why there?'

'I plan to stay there a few days. A Panchayat official was supposed to meet me at the station. Did anyone come?'

'No, no one came. Are you from Madras?'

'Yes.'

'Engineer?'

'Mm ... hmm, no. I've come to carry out some research. I have a grant.'

'Really? Research into what?'

'Folk songs.'

'What do you mean?'

'Don't you know ... folklore.'

'I know only "three nought one, up, down". That's all I know. My wife and children are in Tambaram for the sake of the children's education. So I am all by myself here. I have applied for a transfer. But then the divisional office has to agree. Do you know anyone in the Railways?'

'No, I don't. How does one get to Mempatti from here?'

'Only on foot. Hey, kutti, aren't you going there now?' he called out to the cucumber-seller.

'Yes.'

The stationmaster suddenly remembered something. 'Ah, but the tractor goes to Mempatti, right? Will Marudamuthu come now?'

'No, he comes only late in the evening.'

'Will you take this ayya along with you then?'

'All right. But if I have to carry his luggage will he pay me?'

'I will pay you,' said the passenger.

'How much?'

'Three rupees,' he offered, totally unaware of the local economy and costs.

Blue Shirt cut in. 'I will carry your luggage, ayya.'

'*Ada poda!* Nonsense,' said the stationmaster dismissively. 'You have duties here. The Express is due soon.'

Meanwhile, the young woman, spurred by the thought of earning a whole three rupees, had picked up the passenger's suitcase and balanced it on her head with her cucumber bag on top of it.

'Come along, saar,' she said.

They set off.

Blue Shirt burst out, 'Three rupees is too much, ayya. Three-quarters of a rupee is enough.'

'Pah! It's such a long distance,' protested the woman. 'Come, saar. Good morning, saar.'

She walked ahead and he followed. Presently she stepped into the field bordering the road, displaying a flash of anklets. She walked along the raised ridges of the field. In the standing water alongside, her shadow walked with her, upside down. The mango grove ahead guarded a deep green secret. From a pump set nearby water gushed forth to irrigate the fields.

Palmyra tree sentinels stood guard over the ridges of the field. The blue of the sky above was embellished here and there with cotton wool clouds. 'Tirrick, tirrick,' said a bird. 'Syoo, syoo,' said another. A small, black velvet bird started singing, its tail rising and falling with the cadences of its song. Kalyanaraman thought he could detect a hint of F sharp in those notes. Violins played in his mind.

The young woman turned around. 'You're so slow,' she remarked.

'Wait, wait,' he urged her. 'Don't run.' He stopped and lit a cigarette and walked up to her.

'What caste are you?' asked the woman. 'Are you a Chettiar?'

'I'm a Brahmin.'

'Brahmin? And you are smoking a cigarette? Don't you people shave your head?'

He laughed. 'What's your name?' he asked.

'Vellayamma. People call me Velli.' Then, pointing to his guitar, she asked, 'What's that?'

'A musical instrument.'

'Oh … does it sing?'

'If it is played, it will sing. Do you know any songs?'

'Do you mean cinema songs?'

'No, no, I mean the traditional songs from here.'

'Sometimes I sing them. But he laughs at me when I do.'

'Who?'

'That same one, saar. They told you about him at the station … he drives a *daktar*.'

'Oh, you mean *tractor*. Marudamuthu?'

'Yes, he is the one who drives the daktar. He can also connect electric wires. Like you, he also smokes cigarettes. At the Papparapatti market, with a kerchief around his neck.'

'Your husband?'

'No, saar. But we are going to get married.'

She stepped into the slush and strode along. *Salak … salak*. He looked around for a way to avoid the slush.

'Come along, saar. This is the way.'

He removed his shoes. Tentatively he stepped barefoot into the wet mud … and promptly slipped and fell. He rose, dripping muddy water and oozing sludge. He resorted to an exaggerated gait like a circus clown. Fortunately, the camera had escaped damage. She laughed.

'Your trousers are soaked in mud.'

He did the best he could to wash away the mud in the stagnant water. Now the pathway was less treacherous. As he followed her, he wondered, *how is she able to walk barefoot like this?* His eyes dwelt on the sway of her hips, and he experienced a stab of jealousy towards her intended husband, Marudamuthu.

He adjusted the focus on the camera. 'Velli!' he called out.

She turned.

CLICK!

It was a colour film. Against a lush green background a dark goddess turns and looks at the camera … he prayed that he had set the correct aperture for the shot.

'Did you take a photo?'

'Yes.'

'Of me?'

'Mm.'

'Show me.'

'It won't be ready right away. It will take a few days.'

'Will you take a photo of him and me together?'

'Who?'

'Him. I told you!'

Again Marudamuthu!

Where exactly had they entered Mempatti? Anyway, here they were. On a granite platform at the foot of a large banyan tree, four men sat chatting. When they spotted Velli and Kalyanaraman, they stopped talking and stared. One of them asked, 'Velli, where are you taking him?'

'To our village only.'

Kalyanaraman approached them. 'I am supposed to meet a Panchayat official.'

One of the men, about forty-five years old, with a greying moustache and a chilli-red nose, was clad in a Kamaraj-style shirt. In his pocket was a bunch of dirty scraps of paper clipped together. He said, 'I am a Panchayat official. My name is Pichaipillai. Have you come about a *patta* certificate?'

'No, sir. I am going to stay here for a while. I have a letter addressed to a Panchayat official. It is from the PDO.'

'Ah, yes. Thangarasu Anna was mentioning that someone from Madras is expected.'

'Thangarasu! Yes, that's the name he mentioned. Now I remember. Where can I find him?'

'Here he comes. Enda, dei ...'

'Welcome, welcome! They said you would be coming on Friday.'

'What day is it today?' responded Kalyanaraman.

Thangarasu pondered the question for a moment. 'Yes ... Friday. What an idiot I am. I was thinking all along that it is Thursday!'

'He may even forget his own wife,' teased Pichaipillai. Thangarasu turned angrily towards him, but immediately broke into a smile.

'How did you get here?'

'I walked from the station. Where is that girl?'

Thangarasu called out. 'Hey, Velli, wait there!' Then, turning to Kalyanaraman, he asked, 'Would you like some buttermilk?'

Velli stood waiting. Thangarasu sported slickly combed hair and a slight potbelly encircled with a belt. His shirt looked store-bought. Through the thin cloth of the shirt pocket a packet of Berkeley cigarettes and some rupee notes were visible.

'I heard you are interested in folk music. I've told Periatha about it. She is very good with *oppari* songs which are sung at funerals.' Velli, waiting nearby, laughed. A little boy came and stood in front of Kalyanaraman and stared into his face unblinkingly. He reached out and touched the camera.

'Thangarasu, where is this visitor going to stay?' asked Pichaipillai.

'You know what ... I've cleared out space for him in the zamindar's house.'

'But the whole verandah there is piled with grain.'

The small boy pointed at the camera and asked, 'Will it show cinema?'

One of the men remarked, 'You are taking him there? To the zamin house?'

'Why do you ask?' Kalyanaraman wanted to know. 'What's wrong with the zamin house?'

Thangarasu's response came instantly. 'Nothing, nothing,' he said reassuringly. 'Just come along with me, mister. You fellows just go on gossiping. Here is a visitor who has come all the way from Madras, he is tall. Can he be comfortable in our kind of homes? At the zamin house the irrigation tank is next door, and Marudamuthu has laid wiring for electric lighting. Ayya will be very comfortable there. Let's go, ayya.'

Thangarasu and Kalyanaraman set off along with Velli. The men behind them continued to discuss something in low voices.

'What are they saying?' he asked.

'They will be chattering about this and that. Forget it. Let us just keep walking.'

'Where to?' Velli wanted to know.

'To the zamin house, of course.'

'What? The zamin house?' Velli was startled. She had stood too far away to hear that part of the conversation at the banyan tree.

'Yes. Where's Marudamuthu?'

'He has gone to buy manure.'

Soon they were walking along the only road that the village boasted.

It was lined with coconut-frond-thatched hutments, each revealing an island of darkness inside through its only door. In front of their houses, the womenfolk were fetching water and washing vessels. The brass vessels gleamed with the vigorous scrubbing they had received. There was a neat green square in front of each door. Beyond, in the sand, children were relieving themselves.

A bunch of children were playing a traditional game under a tree ... *vettava kuthava* ... shall I cut, shall I punch. A little further along was an Ayyanar-Kali temple. A moustachioed sepoy and a cement horse stood alongside the sword-wielding valorous figure of Ayyanar, the divine protector of the village. Kalyanaraman glimpsed the prongs of a trident tipped with red, small *sannadhis* for the Snake God, Pillayar and a couple of minor deities. There were two wells and a pond, green-shadowed and strewn with leaves. The image of the temple building swayed in the water in tune with the pond's secret dreams.

When they arrived at the zamin house, Kalyanaraman was astonished. It was a huge house, an incongruous structure in a village so tiny and poor.

'What an enormous house!' he exclaimed. 'Who built this here?'

'The zamindar built it. All this area up to Papparapatti belonged to him. Then the government came and took away most of it. The family moved away somewhere north. The old zamindar died and his educated sons have taken jobs somewhere. The wife, the grandmother … all are dead. The sons have been trying to sell the house, but who is interested in a back-of-beyond village like this? I thought I would buy it myself. I offered them forty thousand, but they are asking for a lakh. I have the key. Will you buy this house?'

'What? Me?' Kalyanaraman laughed at the very thought.

'They say it has three hundred rooms,' said Velli. 'I've never been inside.'

'That's all idle rumour,' said Thangarasu dismissively.

'They also say that in the tamarind tree …'

'Keep quiet!' admonished Thangarasu.

Wild plants were flourishing on the tall outer walls. Past the massive wooden front gates, the path to the house was a mess of overgrown grass, thorny bushes and rubble, leaving barely enough space for a person to make his way through. A stone slab bore the date 1926 carved on it. A domed portico awaited them, with eight steps leading up to a spacious front verandah and three large doors. Inside, above the doorways, glowed decorative semi-circular haloes embedded with red and green glass.

And then came the stairway to an upper floor; then, more stairs to more and more upper floors. At the very top, a pillared courtyard.

In the dilapidated garden stood a statue of an Italian lady, her breast covered with crow droppings. A fountain stood patiently, having stopped working in 1947. A broken-down horse carriage lay tilted over. A dog was sitting inside it.

'Ch … ch … ch … Mani, Mani,' called Velli, using the generic name 'Mani' that all village dogs seemed to share. The dog came out, wagging its tail.

Back at the house, Thangarasu opened the door to a room on the left side of the house. 'It needs a bit of sweeping and cleaning up,' he remarked. 'We were expecting you only tomorrow. I have put a bench in here. And there is an electric lamp too.'

Kalyanaraman entered the room. He felt a chill run down his spine. He was assailed by an unfamiliar, unpleasant sensation.

2

'WELL, MAY I GO now?' asked Thangarasu.

'All right ...'

'What will you do about dinner?'

'I've brought bread and biscuits. If you could just have some milk sent to me ...'

'On a daily basis?'

'Let's see. Let me settle down first.'

'I could bring ayya dinner,' said Velli. 'But he is a Brahmin, so he won't eat meat curry.'

'Don't worry, I'll manage,' Kalyanaraman assured her, handing her three rupees as promised.

Thangarasu was horrified. 'Three rupees? Don't spoil her like this!' he protested.

'Che, she has carried the suitcase such a long distance, Thangarasu. Please come tomorrow morning. I need to meet some people from the village who are familiar with music.'

'I will bring them, ayya. So I will see you tomorrow.'

'I will also leave now, ayya,' said Velli.

Kalyanaraman watched as the two of them walked away. Velli had a spring to her step, and the tinkling sound of her anklets lingered in the air awhile.

Kalyanaraman sank back onto the bench, feeling somewhat overwhelmed. 'My God! I've left civilization far behind and landed up here, virtually a prisoner, in a zamindar's mansion. Now everything is unfamiliar ... new faces, new environment. I've overcome quite a few obstacles to follow my passion for folk music … its lyrics, its musical structure. How many days will I have to spend here?'

Kalyanaraman was unlike other young men. He was an introvert who spent most of his time immersed in his own thoughts. When other young men were taking up college courses in engineering, medicine or law, he had opted for a degree in English literature. When others were writing entrance exams to enter the IAS or to land a plum job at a bank, Kalyanaraman was studying music. When others got married and posed for the photographer's flashbulb, he was studying Tamil literature. He took lessons in Western music from an Anglo-Indian teacher and applied himself to the intricacies of semiquavers and major and minor scales.

He encountered a folk song quite by chance on the Chennai station platform. It was late at night. A woman from Sivagiri who had migrated to Chennai hoping to make her livelihood in that city was singing to her little daughter. The child lay facedown on the platform while the mother patted her back and sang a lullaby:

'*My king, my dear one, my lord,*
Where have you been all this while?
I was hidden during the month of Maasi,
I was swathed in dense rain clouds;
After the month was over
I arrived to visit Mother!'

Kalyanaraman stood mesmerized as he listened to the woman's song. Its sentiment, lyrics and elegance; its universality and popular appeal; its simplicity, its captivating melody …

That was the day Kalyanaraman's folk music odyssey began.

He went to the Tamil Research Centre in Adyar where a professor was collecting folk songs as part of a research grant project. As it happened, the professor needed an assistant. The timing was just right, and Kalyanaraman had found his niche. So here he was on his first research trip.

He opened his suitcase. Cassettes; a tape recorder; shaving items; several strips of tablets of various kinds to cover all health issues that could possibly arise; books to devour; toothpaste; a photo of his late sister; a few pots and pans (he had planned to buy a stove and do some cooking); a small coffee filter; coffee packets; chocolate bars … uh … oh … he could have given Velli some chocolate. He felt a stab of longing in the pit of his stomach.

Click. When she had turned at his call he had clicked a photo. Her glance at that moment was of one who is confident in her own beauty. Oh, the curve of those breasts! They swayed gently with her gait because she wore no inner garment. Who the hell was that wretched Marudamuthu!

When I handed her those three rupees, I could have at least touched her hand …

Such thoughts were visiting Kalyanaraman's mind now after a very long time.

'Che, stop it!' he reprimanded himself. 'I'm here on a different mission.'

He picked up the guitar, tightened its G string and plucked it. 'Daang', it sang in Velli's voice. He dusted off the bench, sat down and played a couple of chords on the guitar. G, A7, G, A7 … the notes resonated in the room. He raised his eyes … and received a jolt. A head had appeared in the window! The moment he realized he had been spotted, the little boy who had been peeping in took to his heels. Kalyanaraman laughed to himself in relief.

He left the room and came out into the hall. A few ancient green chairs stood around. A marble slab bore a *kolam* shaped like a swastika. On a wall hung a framed citation: 'This is a citation of welcome to Maha Sri Papparapatti, Mempatti, Vempatti Zamindar in the poetic format of *aruseergazhi nediladi aasiriya viruttam …*' It was a paean of praise from a long-departed poet to a long-departed zamindar.

Kalyanaraman approached the staircase. A strong odour of bat droppings assailed him. Dust everywhere. He climbed slowly, arriving at a balcony. More steps led upwards. Another floor. And from the head of those, a flight of wooden steps welcomed him. They led up even higher to the topmost domed courtyard. Why not try those too …

'Creech … creech …' the wooden steps creaked and even swayed slightly. He arrived safely at the top near the small *mandapam*. A stiff breeze blew across. In the distance a goods train chugged along. The whole of Mempatti was on view from up here. The pond, the temple. In the far distance, near the banyan tree where he had met Thangarasu, a puff of dust announced the passage of a tractor.

Kalyanaraman decided to explore the mandapam. Built in the shape of a pentagon, it had seating accommodation and floor tiles decorated with kolams. But wait … what were these on the floor? A few cigarette butts! The filter lengths on them were unfamiliar to him. What brand could they be? He picked up one of the butts and looked closely. State Express! Who could be smoking these? In a village like this, inside the decrepit house of a zamindar, and that too right on the top floor, someone smoked State Express cigarettes! It was a mystery!

Now the tractor appeared to be heading straight towards him. He went downstairs and out of the house. Nature's preparations for sunset were visible on the western horizon. Presently, with a noise like a huge metal bird flapping its wings, the tractor came bouncing along. As it came closer, it became clear that there were two people inside. In the bucket seat was a young man; seated on the mudguard of the rear tyre, and clutching the young man firmly was Velli! Kalyanaraman's heart sang.

'You're back again?' he asked Velli.

'My respects, sir,' said the young man. 'I am Marudamuthu.'

'Oh, so you're the one.'

'Velli told me you had arrived.'

Marudamuthu was no taller than Velli.

His black hair was curly and well-groomed, his nose well-shaped. His head rose gracefully from the nape of his neck, and his brow was broad. The muscles of his forearm bulged, a tribute to his hard labour. His chest was like a solid door. He wore a banian with a red top cloth draped over the shoulder. Peacock-feather patterns adorned the border of his dhoti.

Marudamuthu looked directly at Kalyanaraman and asked, 'Are you going to be staying here?' Even as he spoke, his gaze turned towards the tamarind tree abutting the front verandah.

'Yes.'

'For how many days?'

Velli cut in. 'Ayya has come to listen to music. He was telling Thangarasu Ayya about it. He will pay to hear people sing.'

'Oh, that's great!' remarked Marudamuthu. 'Shall I sing a song?'

'Ayye, yes, sing … sing …' urged Velli.

'I'm interested only in folk songs … you know, the traditional songs in your society. What you sing when working in the fields, or at the temple, or during festivals; what you sing to your babies as you rock them in your arms; what you sing at funerals to mourn a soul's passing … these are the kinds of songs I want to hear.'

A … da … who sings that kind of thing these days? wondered Velli. Then, changing the topic, she asked, 'Does the light work?'

'I haven't checked.'

'Let's go and see,' suggested Marudamuthu. 'I'm the one who installed the wiring.'

He led the way back to the house, striding enthusiastically. He entered the room that had been allotted to Kalyanaraman and clicked the switch on the wall. Light! 'Look, pilla!' he boasted to his would-be bride, clicking the switch on and off a few times.

Marudamuthu listed his engineering skills for Kalyanaraman's appreciation. 'I can repair pump motors. I can even do the coil winding on the motors because I went to the town and learnt how to do it. I can change a fuse. I can take that tractor apart and put it together again.'

'I know nothing about such matters,' confessed Kalyanaraman. 'I'm wary of machines of all kinds. Do you work in the fields?'

'Yes, saar, I'm a tenant farmer. I have plans to buy some land of my own soon. But I'm wondering whether to buy a motorcycle first. Those landowners are from Mevaram ... Brahmins like you. They live in Bangalore. They pay no attention to their land. They visit just once a year in the month of Thai to collect the harvested grain. How is that enough?'

'I hear you are going to marry this young woman?'

'Is that what she told you? What a minx! She is the one who is dead set on marrying me!' remarked Marudamuthu rather coarsely.

'Ah ... ah ... don't you dare!' scolded Velli in mock anger. 'I'll throw a rock at you and that will be the end of you. Beware!'

'She already has a cousin who would be the obvious choice of a husband, except that he is so short that he barely comes up to her waist. So now she is throwing herself at me. I have marriage offers from Muthiapuram, Pandiapuram ... so many places ...'

'Hold on! There's no way I'm going to marry this madman!' fumed Velli.

Marudamuthu roared with laughter. 'See how quickly she has lost her temper! No, no, saar, I am making a solemn pledge. Once the harvest is over, I will marry this girl. She is mine. In any case she has made me stand in chest-deep water and swear an oath!'

Marudamuthu's gaze fell on the guitar. 'Huh …? What is this?'

'It's a musical instrument.'

'Very neat and compact! Made from jackfruit-tree wood?' He picked it up carefully and plucked a string.

Twang!

'It sings! Do you play this?'

'And what's this?' Marudamuthu had spotted something sitting next to the guitar.

'It's a tape recorder.'

'Ah, yes! I've seen something like this in the town. If you talk into it, it talks back. Right? Velli, come and look at this.'

Marudamuthu turned on the recorder.

'Ayya took a photo of me,' declared Velli.

'Oh, really? Will you take one of me too, ayya?' asked Marudamuthu.

'He said he would take a photo of the two of us together,' Velli informed him.

Marudamuthu rewound the tape and turned on the 'play' button. The recorder repeated their latest conversation.

Velli was astounded. Her eyes widened and shone with excitement. '*Athaadi*! It is repeating what you and I said! Who is inside that box?' she demanded.

'There's no one inside the box, you silly thing. Look … do you see this tape? What we speak goes and sticks to the tape. Isn't that so, saar?'

'Yes, yes,' agreed Kalyanaraman. 'Sing a song, Velli.'

'Do they make these recorders in our country?' Marudamuthu wanted to know.

'Yes, they do. Please tell Velli to sing a song.'

'Go on, sing, pilla!'

'Mm ... I don't know any song.'

'*Adei*, sing something. Ayya is asking you. What about that song you were singing when we were coming back from the market? Sing that one.'

'You will laugh at me.'

'I will go away into the other room. But you must sing. She knows plenty of songs, saar. Periatha has taught her lots of them.' Marudamuthu left the room.

With great reluctance, obvious embarrassment and much glancing at the floor near her feet, Velli started singing in a soft, childish voice.

'One who has read the page of a book,
One whose hand has held a pen,
One who has studied the Bharatham,
Such a one have I not seen for many a day.'

'Shabash!' exclaimed Kalyanaraman. Overcome with shyness, Velli covered her face with her hands. Kalyanaraman had detected shades of the Nadanamakriya ragam in that tune. She had rendered it in perfect pitch. 'You have a good voice,' he told her. He reached out and plucked a string on the guitar. As the sound resonated, he urged her, 'Now let me see if you can sing something in this pitch.'

With absolute ease her voice glided into that minor chord.

'He has betel-stained teeth,
And a spendthrift he is;
To measure the paddy of Mevaram
How much he spends!!'

'Beautiful! This is it!' exclaimed Kalyanaraman. 'Marudamuthu, come here, she was singing about you.'

Marudamuthu entered. 'I heard what she sang,' he said. 'Now listen to this.' He began reciting:

'I will give you auspicious turmeric root,
I will give you a blouse for your breast;
Cuddle me, snuggle with me,
I will give you a child to caress.'

He stopped and roared with laughter. Red in the face with embarrassment, Velli turned and ran out of the room.

Kalyanaraman turned off the recorder. 'Why did you chase her away like that when things were going so well?'

'I'll sing instead, saar. Record me. I'll sing "Ennadi Meenakshi" ...'

'Shut up! Go away now. You can come back later.'

'You don't mind sleeping all by yourself here at night? Shall I come and keep you company?'

'I will be fine.'

'All right, so I'll leave now,' said Marudamuthu, turning and walking away. '*Adiyoi*,' he called out to Velli. 'You maiden adorned with bangles, you woman in a *valathattu* sari ... wait for me, di.'

Velli was waiting near the tractor. Kalyanaraman watched as Marudamuthu put his arms around Velli and lifted her onto the tractor. A jolt of something very much like jealousy went through him as he watched.

Later, in the light of a single electric bulb (courtesy of Marudamuthu), Kalyanaraman ate bread with mixed fruit jam. It was pitch-dark outside. Frogs croaked, the local *thirugu* insects chirped. Oh … and what was that? Was it a sound? Or was it just the sound of silence?

Kalyanaraman turned on the tape recorder.

'*Ayya took a photograph of me …*'

And later, in her tuneful, childish voice:

'*One who has read the page of a book,*
One whose hand has held a pen …'

He listened to Velli's song three times and copied the lyrics in his notebook. He deleted the poem that Marudamuthu had recited by recording over the tape.

He then took out another cassette and slotted it into the recorder. Turn it on …

'*Money, Money, Money,*
It's kind of funny
In a rich man's world!'

Rich man … like Maharaja Sri Zamindar. The one in whose house, on the topmost floor, lay the stubs of State Express cigarettes. Recent memories crowded his mind, along with other images.

'*Did you come on the three nought one?*'

'*She's meant for me.*'

'*Velli!*' *CLICK*! Her checked sari unwinds from her body in slow motion. *CLICK*! *CLICK!* '*Lie down, Velli.*' *CLICK!*

'*Cuddle me, snuggle with me,*
I'll give you a child to caress.'

'*Come here, Velli. No, no, don't go to that dark fellow.*'

Che! He dissolved the mental images and immersed himself in a book.

He read:

'Nowadays even for the oral tradition to continue, the written word has become necessary. There is a traditional type of folk music called "*kolai chindu*" which continues to flourish in the northern regions of the Tamil land. They are songs about murders, set against the backdrop of society ...'

When exactly did he go to sleep? And why now had he woken with a start? He was soaked in sweat; he was unused to sleeping with no ceiling fan. The frogs still croaked. The insects continued to chirp. But what was that other sound? It came from upstairs.

3

THOSE SOUNDS WERE DEFINITELY coming from upstairs. Someone was moving chairs around. Kalyanaraman could not summon up the courage to get up and investigate. He turned on the light and checked his watch. One-fifteen. He lay on his back for a while, staring at a crossbeam on the ceiling. Teak rafters painted saffron threw lines of shadows on the walls. The chandelier, festooned with cobwebs, had no bulbs. Marudamuthu's single electric bulb swayed slightly as it hung on its long wire. Outside the window, a pale Krishna paksha moon, midway in its cycle between new and full, had made the garden keep unnecessary secrets. Dark patches of shadows here and there lent an aura of surrealism to the scene.

Kalyanaraman could not get back to sleep. He got up and turned on the radio that was part of his two-in-one recorder. On the 31-metre band, radio stations crackled. A voice from West Germany was complaining about the problem caused by refugees from Yugoslavia and Turkey. The BBC declared, 'This is Our World'; China offered plaintive music to the airwaves; Moscow declared that every citizen of their country was prosperous. How many voices at this hour! So many night owls! Was one of those voices coming from inside the house? From upstairs? An actual voice … or just a noise?

He turned down the volume on the radio … and gasped in shock. The sound now came from the stairway … the sound of footsteps descending, unhurriedly, deliberately. The joints and nails of the ancient wooden steps creaked and squeaked in protest. Kalyanaraman froze in fear. The door to his room was locked from inside; but one strong kick from the other side would be enough to force it open.

The footsteps were approaching his room. Slowly but relentlessly. Yes, his room was the target. The footsteps came to a halt outside the door. Whoever it was stood at the threshold.

Silence. A long, long silence. In Kalyanaraman's case, a silence accompanied by an adrenaline-fuelled tension that made his hair stand on end.

He reached out and turned up the volume on the radio. He did not want to hear the sound of tapping on the door. Pop music burst forth from the radio. Kalyanaraman's lips, however, sought comfort in Sanskrit.

Bhayakrith bhayanashanaha …

He is the one who can cause fear; He is also the one who can destroy fear.

Kalyanaraman plucked up some courage. He turned off the radio. Silence. One minute … nothing. Ten minutes … now, a whole half-hour. Still nothing but silence.

First, he would have to get himself a flashlight. And also a weapon of some kind. He must check with Thangarasu about it tomorrow. Maybe someone was living upstairs and Thangarasu forgot to tell him about it. Well, he would ask him tomorrow. Tomorrow … but right now he would try to sleep.

He inserted a cassette of soothing violin music into the tape recorder and set it at a low volume. He lay back and closed his eyes.

He saw his sister's face. The doctor had said, 'Vellore is the best hospital for open-heart surgery, but it will cost fifteen thousand rupees. Otherwise it will have to be at this other hospital. Anyway, you have to decide quickly.' Before they could decide, God decided to take her. 'Anna, will you buy that blue sari for me?' she had asked. But there was no time for that … too late …

The notes of Mancini's violin rushed into his ears and invaded his soul. He slept.

Birds he had never met in his city were now calling him by name to wake him. 'Kalyanaraman! Kalyanaraman!' they chirped. He awoke. Everything looked very different in the morning. Under the light of the early sun, all of last night's secrets and fears had slunk into hiding. Through the window, the morning light dusted gold upon him with no heat.

He stepped out of the house and spotted the pump set a little distance away. He went back inside, collected soap and toothpaste and an empty jerrycan, and set out towards the pump. As he entered a grove of trees, fallen leaves crunched under his feet. His cheerful mood was fully restored.

Inside a brick-walled room with a tin roof weighted down with stones to prevent errant gusts of wind from blowing it away, the pump growled mightily and gushed a huge spout of water into the fields. He sat under that flood and started a refreshing bath. 'Tit … tit … tit … tiralalalooba … tit … tit,' he sang, a song with no words.

He heard laughter behind him. Struck numb with shock, he let the soap slip out of his hands. He turned his head. There stood Velli with another young woman, towels draped over their shoulders.

'Wha … at!' stuttered Kalyanaraman.

'You came here to bathe?' asked Velli's companion, averting her eyes from Kalyanaraman.

'Why, what's wrong?'

'This is the bathing place for women,' she informed him.

'Oh, sorry!' he exclaimed, springing to his feet. He sat down again immediately, realizing he was wearing only wet underwear.

The two women laughed again and turned their backs.

'Please move away a little. I will leave now.'

'Do you see that hand pump and tap? You could have your bath there.'

Kalyanaraman hurriedly put on his trousers and shirt, and with his hair still dripping wet, he turned to leave. As he crossed the spot where the two women were standing, Velli's friend let out a screech of laughter that grated on him. Velli admonished her friend, 'Tha! Keep quiet!' But she too was laughing.

After he had walked away a few steps, he realized he had left his soap behind. Instinctively he turned. A tantalizing glimpse of Velli's bare bosom. Afraid to stop and stare he turned abruptly and hurried away.

Back at the zamin house Thangarasu was waiting for him along with an elderly lady.

'You've had your bath? What's your plan for coffee and breakfast? I've brought some milk,' said Thangarasu.

'Thangarasu, who is this amma?'

'This is Periatha. I told you about her yesterday.' The old woman had opened the drawstrings on her betelnut pouch to take out a wad of chewing betel. She acknowledged the introduction with a slight smile. Her hair was bundled carelessly on her head. Restless eyes, a lined forehead, just one or two red-stained teeth left in her mouth. She was probably around sixty. Yet, in that near-toothless smile and that imperious nose there was something attractive.

'Please sit,' invited Kalyanaraman. 'I'll be back soon.'

'I have to go, saar,' said Thangarasu. 'Periatha, this ayya has come from Madras. Listen carefully to what he says.' She nodded, busily chewing on a wad of betel leaf.

'Saar, you have to speak louder. She is totally deaf in one ear.'

'Thangarasu, just one more thing. Is there anyone else staying in this house?'

'No, why do you ask?'

'In the night I heard someone moving around.'

'Where?'

'Upstairs.'

'Did you hear anklets tinkling?'

'No, it sounded like a man walking around.'

'Did you feel scared?'

'Well, not exactly, but since I was alone ...'

Thangarasu pondered awhile. 'Maybe some of the fellows who work in the fields had too much to drink and wandered into the house ... Did you hear anyone talking?'

'No.'

'Hm. Anyway, at night you should close the entrance gate to the garden. This morning I found it wide open. I will ask Marudamuthu to come and stay with you at night.'

'All right,' accepted Kalyanaraman.

Thangarasu cast a bemused glance around the house. *Who could it have been*, he muttered to himself. As he was leaving he saw what Periatha had been up to while the two of them had been talking.

'Ey, old woman, so you're already up to your usual tricks ...'

Periatha had collected a lapful of guavas, drumsticks and unripe mangoes.

'They were all going waste anyway.'

Thangarasu scolded her. 'You shouldn't have plucked them. This place is my responsibility. Put them all down immediately.' He added a word of caution to Kalyanaraman. 'Ayya, keep a close eye on her. If she's left to herself she will strip the whole garden. And don't leave any loose change lying around. She's a thief.'

'Ayya!' exclaimed Periatha in mock protest. When Thangarasu had left, she smiled at Kalyanaraman and remarked, 'You look very noble. Are you a prince?'

'Wait here, I'll come back.'

'Is there any coffee?'

'I myself haven't had anything yet,' he replied, as he turned and left the room.

The milk that Thangarasu had brought was still hot. He spooned in some sugar and Bru, stirred it and gulped it down. The rich milk made his stomach uneasy. He lit a cigarette. When he came back, he found Periatha seated in the verandah with her fruit collection laid out in front of her.

'They're all going to waste. Only the squirrels are eating them. What's wrong if I take a few? Are you family?'

'What?'

'Do you belong to the zamindar's family?'

'No, I came to listen to songs.'

'Eh ...?'

'Folk songs ... your songs ...'

'Eh ...?'

He remembered she was hard of hearing.

'Songs. Folk songs!' he shouted.

'Ah ... I know all the songs. Tell me, how old am I? I was born in the month of Panguni.'

'I don't know ... how old are you?'

'Forty, saar.'

'Oh, you should be acting in cinemas. What songs do you know?'

'I know all of them ... oppari, *kodangi*, *kalakam* ... they said you would pay money for the songs ... One rupee will get me some *malli* coffee, a measure of rice and some chewing tobacco. I have a son, but he doesn't give me any money. And that stingy wife of his won't offer me even water. It's ages since I had a nice sari to wear. Look at this one ... all tattered ...'

'Ey, ey, don't cry!'

'My husband's gone, saar. It's been three years now. He worked in the fields. One day he came home and said he wanted to go to the latrine. But suddenly he just fell over. He didn't open his eyes. At the big hospital they gave him an injection in the back. Such a big injection it was. That mean daughter-in-law of mine was pregnant. Could he not at least have lived to see his grandson? But no ... he never opened his eyes again. He was big and strong like you. Now I have nowhere to go. Neither my mother's home nor my husband's home.

'*In a train did I travel towards my mother's home;*
But no shelter did I find there, it was no longer mine.'

Kalyanaraman was wonderstruck. 'Wait, wait!' he urged her. He hurried inside, fetched the tape recorder and set it up. 'Now sing that again.'

She wiped her eyes. 'Will you give me money?'

Kalyanaraman handed her five rupees. 'I don't have any change,' she said.

'That's all right. Keep it all.'

Her sorrow vanished like a summer shower. She sniffed and remarked, 'What's that scent here? You have applied *masi pachai* herbs on your body.' She had detected Kalyanaraman's perfume.

'It's just the scent I use. Forget that, just sing now.'

'What's this box, saar?'

'A tape recorder.'

'Huh!?'

'I'll show you later. But first you must sing.'

'*Look over there, do you see Annaachi's mandapams?*
Under one of the mandapams I was held prisoner
Yes, my pea-hen-like self was trapped there
And they did not care
That I was a pea-hen.
They came and shot an arrow at me ...'

'Beautiful! World class! I love you!' shouted Kalyanaraman in sheer delight.

'*Sita was born at the foothills of Chinna Madurai;*

The tears she wept filled her lap and overflowed
To flood the whole of Thirupparkadal.'

Such beautiful lines of song were lying buried in this village! Where had they come from? How had they spread? For a moment Kalyanaraman was in the presence of God himself. The tape recorder spun hungrily and saved up every word and note of Periatha's songs.

'Ayya, will you come to the village?' Marudamuthu asked from the window. He entered the house freely and examined Kalyanaraman's shaving kit. He picked up the shaving soap and examined it. He shook the aftershave lotion experimentally.

'How will we get to the village?'

'In the tractor. You will like the ride. There will be some mud thrown up, so wear your dark glasses. Also dark pants if you have any. I heard you went to bathe in the women's bathing area. Velli told me.'

'Oh, so she has told you already!'

'I'll come back at night to sleep here. I heard you had a scare last night.'

'I wasn't afraid or anything like that ...'

'City people are easily frightened, saar. There is a vampire living in that tamarind tree. Velli has seen it. One night I came with a torch to confront it. It laughed loudly *bihi* ... *bihi* ... *bihi* ... and fled. We have to be brave, saar. See, this is a charm that the *archakar* at the Muthamma temple gave me. It protects people from harmful spirits. Inside is a paste made from the burnt hair of a woman. Did I frighten you? Your trousers are wet ...'

Kalyanaraman was annoyed. 'Che, no, that can leaks,' he explained.

'Ah, so that's what it is! Shall we go then?'

Soon, Kalyanaraman, seated in the side seat of the tractor, was being thrown up and down and side to side. With every bump on the road, his bones rattled as though they had a life of their own, and the flesh on his face vibrated in tune with the tractor's noisy engine. In the shade of the trees, babies slept blissfully in their cloth hammock cradles. The fields offered rear views of women, bent over as they tended to the crops.

Velli appeared on the roadside and signalled the tractor to a stop. 'Will you buy me something?' she asked Marudamuthu.

'Oh, sure, pilla, I'll buy you cotton candy.'

'Ayye!'

He pinched her cheek playfully. 'Wait near the chrysanthemum bush. I will drop ayya off and meet you there. We can drive north.'

'No, I won't come.'

'Yes, you are coming.'

'Only after Thai.'

'We can go to the cinema tent. You can munch *thuvarangai*.'

Kalyanaraman cut in. 'Marudamuthu … are we going to be stopping here for a long time …?'

'No, no, saar. We will go. I'll see you later, pilla.'

Kalyanaraman scolded himself. 'Why? Why do I feel this way? Why such jealousy? Am I not here only because I am in love with folk music?'

His eyes dwelt on Velli as she gazed longingly at the departing tractor. He looked till he lost sight of her in a billowing cloud of dust.

They entered the town. There was dust everywhere. They went past Bhuvaneswari Cinema Hall, a loudspeaker store named Anna Light and Sound, and a cycle shop. Kalyanaraman noticed a jaggery market, mounds of chillies and bales of coarse handloom cloth. Vasantha Lodge appeared just before the town bus stand. The walls everywhere seemed to be covered with posters advertising eczema medications.

Kalyanaraman bought a small kerosene stove and a flashlight. When he was buying soap, he was reminded of Velli.

He bought a string of plastic beads and handed them to Marudamuthu. 'Give these to Velli,' he said.

'Ade! I was thinking I will get a dot-print sari for her. But this is very nice too. I'm sure she will like it. She will agree to come to the cinema tent with me,' said Marudamuthu with a meaningful wink.

Once more that dagger of jealousy ...

On the way back from the town, when the tractor was driving past Thirunilam Station, Kalyanaraman caught sight of a young woman.

4

THE YOUNG WOMAN RAN towards the tractor. She thumbed a lift, using the modern gesture of a raised thumb. 'Marudamuthu, wait! Wait!' she called out. Her voice was drowned in the roar of the tractor engine. As the tractor turned the corner of the road, Kalyanaraman saw her standing and staring after the disappearing vehicle with hands on hips, a picture of frustration. The next moment she was lost to view.

Kalyanaraman was unaware that destiny would bring her into his path in the future. For now, he merely wondered idly who she was, and then forgot about the incident. The afternoon sun was blazing down from the western sky when they made their way back to Mempatti. Velli ran out onto the road and blocked their path. She looked weary, covered in sweat and dirt after toiling in the fields for hours.

'What did you buy for me?'

'Look, here's a pretty string of beads for you. Ayya picked it out.'

'So *you* didn't buy anything for me?'

'Where do I have the time for shopping? Here, take it.'

Velli's expression revealed her annoyance and disappointment. She snatched the bead necklace from Marudamuthu's hand and flung it back at him.

'Here … take it and wear it yourself!' she fumed.

'Adei … so angry, are you?'

'What do you think? I asked you to buy something for me out of affection. Instead you made ayya buy the gift. May you be cursed! May you be bitten by snakes!'

She walked alongside the slow-moving tractor, continuing her tirade. 'He is a stranger after all. When I went to the market, didn't I buy you that dhoti with the special border? And that thing that goes *click-click* to light your cigarette? You're telling me you had no time? What did you do? Were you leering at some woman in the town?'

Marudamuthu was enjoying her show of temper. He laughed. 'Look how she is scolding me even before we are married!' he said to Kalyanaraman. 'The other day I was talking to a woman social worker. This one here was dying of jealousy. Hey, Velli, still angry? Why do you need a bead necklace at all? Isn't a smile from me enough?'

'Masi pachai! Get lost!'

But she scrambled onto the tractor.

Kalyanaraman remembered how she had scolded Marudamuthu, called him names. But the way her eyes always sought him out ... in the meeting of their glances, in every detail of their body language, he read mutual passion. 'Oh, when can we be together, when can we be one,' they both thought, even when their lips were saying other words.

Kalyanaraman was beginning to hate Marudamuthu.

'Come along,' he urged, 'don't waste time chit-chatting. I have work to do.'

When they returned to the zamin house, they found a bunch of children playing in the garden. Velli got down from the tractor. Marudamuthu shouted at the children, 'Hey, you useless kids, go away ... go!'

'*Ai*, it's the tractor man! Tractor man, tractor man!' chanted the children in chorus.

'Run away now, you accursed rascals. Otherwise I'll knock out all your teeth!'

'Hold on!' urged Kalyanaraman. He went into the house and fetched a piece of chocolate for each of the children. It was as if someone had lit a fuse under them; they erupted in joy.

'Come tomorrow,' Kalyanaraman told them. 'I'll teach you some songs.'

They shouted gleefully as they ran out through the gate.

'They don't know how to sing,' remarked Marudamuthu. 'Those boys are just cowherds.'

'I will make them sing, just watch,' declared Kalyanaraman. 'There is music hidden somewhere deep inside those children. For instance, Velli sings well …'

'See, pilla, ayya says you sing well.'

'Why don't *you* tell me that?'

'I'll come back to sleep here, saar. Velli, ayya was frightened last night so he asked me to sleep here with him. Will you also come?'

'Pah! What cheek!' said Velli huffily.

Kalyanaraman wanted to tell Marudamuthu not to come for the night. Somehow he could not do so. He wanted to talk to Velli alone, but could not think of a way to make that happen. Marudamuthu and Velli left together. Again those little rituals were played out; as they walked away, he was teasing her, and she moved away from him, only to drift closer within a few steps. Even after they were out of sight, the sound of their laughter reached him. *That fellow may have touched her inappropriately … maybe he … Che! I must stop this obsession. Forget! Stop feeling anything, be numb …*

He went into his room. He took out all the things he had bought that day, and arranged them carefully. He wanted to hear Velli's voice. He tapped the 'play' button of the recorder.

'*Sita's birthplace …*' It was Periatha.

He pressed rewind. Play. '*I will bring you fresh turmeric …*' It was Marudamuthu.

Kalyanaraman turned off the recorder.

The evening light still lingered. Why not go upstairs? He climbed slowly and carefully. On the first floor was a large hall, visible through a window. But the door was padlocked. He took a closer look at the lock. The screws that held the hasp in place seemed to be loose. A mere rattling of the door would displace those screws. Someone had tried to open that door; or someone had succeeded in opening it and had then left it shut this way to avoid detection. He took a ballpoint pen from his pocket and tried to open the lock. It gave way instantly!

He entered the hall. A strand of cobweb brushed his face. Dust everywhere, accumulated over many years. Teak furniture ... chairs, tables, sofas ... all covered with dust cloths; an ormolu clock; a six-foot-tall, enlarged photograph of a man. He was big and burly. He wore a turban, a *pottu* on his forehead, and a luxuriant moustache. He was clad in a long coat. A slim silver chain emerged from a button of the coat and disappeared into an inner pocket. He stood next to some faintly seen tallish prop, on top of which was a pile of four or five red books. The man's arm rested on the books, and his eyes gazed forward at the camera. The background was some sort of landscape.

Maybe this was the zamindar?

Nearby was another photo. This time a woman. She was adorned with rich, heavy jewellery. Her nose, ears, neck, arms and waist all displayed elaborate gold ornaments embedded with diamonds and other precious stones. She wore a fussy, puffy blouse. She stared at the camera as though petrified with fear. This must be the wife.

There were also some Ravi Varma paintings, intricately carved teak cupboards and large mirrors that had long lost their silver coating.

Wait ... what was this! The door of one of the cupboards stood ajar. Kalyanaraman stepped up for a closer look. A strong odour of rat droppings emanated from the ancient books that lay inside, along with papers that looked as if they would crumble at a touch. But had all of them been left undisturbed? No! In the layer of dust at one spot, there were distinct fingerprints! He picked up a notebook and turned the pages. On the yellowed pages appeared various notations and entries made with a wooden pen dipped in burnt coal-ash, in a slanting hand. '17-2-6', 'patta', '*dargas*', 'minor suit' and other phrases he could make nothing of. On another page, '... to Ratnavathy my nose pin, anklets and forty *paun* worth of silver coins.'

'Hey!'

Kalyanaraman was startled. He turned. A woman stood in the doorway.

In the shock of this totally unexpected interruption, Kalyanaraman let the old notebook slip from his hand. As it fell to the floor, a flower that had been pressed between its pages way back in 1936 slid out and crumbled to dust.

The woman looked around and walked towards him in a leisurely fashion. It was the same woman he had seen earlier in the day ... the one who had tried to stop them on the street when they were returning from their shopping trip to the town. What was she doing here? Her outfit was ultramodern ... big-city stuff, all of it. She wore a man's shirt and faded jeans; her eyebrows were pencilled and arched. A modest-sized bosom, and hair that had received much attention with shampoo. Her nose and small lips reminded Kalyanaraman vaguely of some flowers he had seen on the trip back to the house.

'You ... you are ...?'

'My name is Snehalatha. And you are ...?'

'Kalyanaraman. Pleased to meet you.'

'My brothers used to call me "Snake". In college I was "Latha". What are you doing, digging around here?'

'Well, I ... I mean ... that is, I ...'

Thangarasu appeared. 'There's a complication,' he remarked. 'Amma has come.'

Casually examining the dark red varnish on her fingernails, Snehalatha suggested, 'First tell him who this "amma" is, Thangarasu.'

'Amma belongs to the zamindar's family, saar. She is the *chinna* zamindar's youngest daughter. Isn't that right, amma?'

'Exactly!' Turning towards the photograph of the burly gentleman, she called out, 'Hi, grandfather!' Maharaja Sri Durairaja did not respond.

'Is that so! I'm so glad!' exclaimed Kalyanaraman.

'Weren't you the one clattering by on the tractor earlier today? Could you not have stopped for a moment when I asked for a lift? I had to walk all the way. My thighs are sore. I have to rub Vaseline on them.'

'Oh, I didn't know you were headed here.'

'Well, here I am. And here I am going to stay. This is my house.'

'Oh …'

'Why have you come to this village? Thangarasu says you are looking for folk songs?'

'Yes, ma'am, I'm researching folk music.'

'Come on! Enough of all the "ma'am" talk. So when you were digging into the things in this cupboard,' she accompanied the words with an energetic mime of digging, 'you were doing "research"?'

'Che, che! Don't misunderstand me. I was feeling bored …'

'The hall was locked,' pointed out Thangarasu.

'The moment I touched it, the lock opened,' explained Kalyanaraman.

Snehalatha was sceptical. 'It just opened! Just like that!'

Then after a pause, 'Are you a Brahmin?'

'Yes.'

'I am from a royal family. Royal lineage, you understand? Oh, what a hole this is! How am I ever going to live here! Jee … sus!!'

That was Thangarasu's cue. 'That was what I was also wondering. Only saar's room has an electric light.'

'Thangarasu, just because we family people don't visit here often, you just went ahead and decided to open up the house to anyone and everyone who comes by! Isn't that so? Do you think this is a *chathram*?'

'Amma, please don't say that. I had no idea you were planning to come. Was there a letter ...?'

'I'm sorry.'

'Just give me a little time. I'll send this casual visitor packing.'

'Don't be angry, ayyare,' said Snehalatha coyly.

'Forgive me, saar. She turned up suddenly. I've seen her long ago as a child. But look, she has her grandmother's nose.' Thangarasu pointed to the photograph of the heavily bedecked woman. Snehalatha looked at the likeness of her ancestor. 'This one? She looks like Pasupaleti Kannamba, the film actress. Who is she, Thangarasu? My grandmother?'

'She is the one who gave birth to your father.'

'What sparklers, I say! That looks like at least a ton of jewellery that she's wearing. What do you think, Kalyanaraman?'

'Well, it makes you wonder how she could even walk around with that much jewellery on her.'

'Thangarasu, get the room opposite this ayya's room ready for me to stay. Okay? That way it will be some security for me here.'

'Security for you? Ayya himself is scared. He says he heard sounds in the night.'

'Oh ... then I will give security to him! Sir, are you married?'

'No.'

'Don't try any tricks on me, okay?'

'Okay,' said Kalyanaraman, laughing.

'You two are talking in English,' remarked Thangarasu with a sheepish smile. It seemed to Kalyanaraman that Thangarasu was gazing rather improperly at Snehalatha. His eyes lingered on the undone top button of her shirt.

They descended the stairs. 'I'm thinking I'll stay for a week or so. I was wondering where to go on vacation. My mother suggested I should come here and take a look at our zamin house to see if everything is okay. So, as you would put it, *odi vanden*, I ran right over here.'

'You travelled here alone?'

'I'll be travelling alone to London next month, my good man! So why not to Mempatti!'

Her suitcase stood in the doorway.

'Mr Kalyanaraman, don't worry. I'm not going to chase you away. Go ahead and do your research.'

'You're teasing me.'

'No, no. Folk music is very important. Thangarasu, come along, let us go and take a look around the village. Arrange for a light in my room ... you mentioned a Marudamuthu ... tell him. Also, we have to get a tape-woven cot, or maybe rope instead of tape ...? And ... by the way, is there a bathroom?'

'Hee, hee ... no, no bathroom.'

'What! So if I need to go I have to go and squat in the fields? My God!'

'There's a separate room over there. We can bring in a couple of buckets of water. You can have a bath there. During the zamindar's time there was a latrine, but it hasn't been used since then. We can have it repaired.'

Kalyanaraman watched as the two of them walked away into the garden. She had a boyish frame; only the hips were a giveaway. Suddenly she leapt up and plucked two guavas from a hanging branch. As she bit into one of them, she turned and called out, 'Kalyanaraman ... catch!' She flung the other guava with such force that it landed with a painful thump on Kalyanaraman's chest as he stood there entirely unprepared for such a test of his alertness. Her laughter echoed in the fading light of late evening.

He stood outside the door till the fading light had deepened into inky darkness. Then he went back into his room, lit the stove and heated some water. He added rice to the boiling water. Then he turned on the tape recorder, selected Periatha's songs and wrote down the lyrics of the songs in a notebook. In a corner of the room stood an empty Crocin tin. If he could attach a stick to it and get some coir string to tie on, it could become a double-bass musical instrument. He could teach those boys how to play it when they came next. Or he could show it to Velli.

Velli had referred to him as a stranger. He had picked out those beads for her in the shop, and she had flung them contemptuously back into the tractor when she realized that Marudamuthu had not selected them. Velli's behaviour rankled with him. He picked up his guitar and played a few notes. With the fingers of his left hand settling familiarly into the appropriate frets, he played Jose Feliciano's interpretation of 'Malaguena'. He imagined he could feel Velli in those Mexican beats.

'Clap, clap!' He was startled by the sound of loud clapping. Snehalatha stood in the doorway of the room.

'Beautiful! You play very well, ayyare!' She strolled in calmly and sat on the floor near him. Looking directly at him, she said, 'I need to ask you something.'

'What is it?'

'Folk music? Pah! Whom are you trying to deceive? Why are you really here? Come clean!'

5

'I DON'T UNDERSTAND WHAT you mean,' protested Kalyanaraman.

'If you want to pretend that you don't understand me, then you won't.'

'Che, no. What do you mean? The purpose of my visit here is really to research folk music. Nothing else. Look at these pages; I've started writing my thesis. I've recorded folk songs on the tape recorder. What else do you think brings me here?'

Snehalatha was thoughtful for a while. Then she said abruptly, 'Forget it. I was just joking. Do you know how to play "Petite Fleur"?'

'Yes, I do,' he replied, and picked out the notes on a single string on the guitar.

'La ... la ... ya ... la ... ta ... ra ... ra ... rum ...' Snehalatha sang the tune without the lyrics. He picked out the tempo of the rhythm on the guitar. She stood and started swaying to the beat in a gentle dance. Her movements were elegant and refined with no hint of vulgarity. Kalyanaraman was enjoying it.

She stopped and remarked, 'You play very well. Let me see your hand.'

He held out his hand. The guitar strings had left marks on his fingertips. She brushed the calluses gently with her own fingertips.

A voice from outside the door. 'Namaskaram!' Marudamuthu had arrived. He introduced himself to Snehalatha.

'Hi, Marudamuthu, Thangarasu told me about you.'

'I've come to set up an electric light in your room, amma. I've also brought a rope cot, a mat and a few other things. I'm going to sleep here tonight for ayya's security. I'm happy you could come. Are your parents well?'

'Oh, yes.'

'Are you a palmist?'

'No, why do you ask?'

'You were looking at ayya's hand, so ...'

'I was looking at his hand to find out how he could play the guitar so beautifully.'

'His hands will be soft. Mine are rough with all the heavy farming work.'

Marudamuthu continued to gaze steadily at her. 'Are you the zamindar's granddaughter?'

'Yes.'

'I can see it in your face.'

'What ...?'

'The family resemblance is there. Your grandfather is very highly respected here. Many of the people here are those who worked on his lands. They still remember those times. They say that he had chariots and that White men would often visit to go hunting. How are you ...?'

'I'm doing fine, Marudamuthu.'

Indicating Kalyanaraman, Marudamuthu said, 'Maybe ayya can move to a place in the town. It may be more convenient for you ...'

'That's not necessary. It's already been decided that ayya will stay in this room and I will take the one on the opposite side. Will you fit up a light for me there?'

The rice boiling on the stove gave out an aroma.

'Kalyanaraman, you even know how to cook!?'

'Well, I can boil rice, and then there is always bread. And pickles, appalam, curds.'

'I have some biscuits. Would you like some?'

'If you will share my *thayir saadam* I will take some of your biscuits.'

Marudamuthu reassured Snehalatha, 'You don't have to go to any trouble. Tomorrow I'll ask Velli to come here and cook meat curry for you. You eat meat, don't you? Ayya here is from an upper caste so he won't touch meat.'

'Who is Velli?' Snehalatha wanted to know.

Kalyanaraman was quick with a reply. He explained in English, 'His girlfriend. Sweet girl.'

'What did he tell you?' asked Marudamuthu.

Snehalatha translated. 'He said she is your friend and a very sweet girl.'

'Marudamuthu is going to marry Velli,' added Kalyanaraman.

'Let that be, saar. That's not going to happen anytime soon. I have potential brides in ten other places anyway.'

'Will you ask her to come tomorrow? I want to see this girl that ayya describes as "sweet".'

'All right.'

Marudamuthu kept trying to engage Snehalatha in conversation. He asked her random questions and told her about himself. 'Tomorrow morning please come to the orchard. I'll give you tender coconut and mangoes. This year I'm the one who is going to clear the weeds from all the fields. Singlehandedly I will drive the tractor over the whole area and plough it. I can lay eight men low with a twirl of my stout stick. I'm keen to learn English. Will you teach me?'

While he talked, Marudamuthu connected a long wire between Kalyanaraman's room and Snehalatha's room opposite. He hung an electric lightbulb. He picked up the rope-woven cot, carried it into her room on one arm, and set it up. When Snehalatha made a move towards her suitcase, Marudamuthu beat her to it and grabbed it first.

'For generations my family has worked for your family, ma,' he told her. 'Will I not carry your luggage?'

Kalyanaraman started wondering whether Marudamuthu had some hidden agenda here, other than just being helpful out of goodwill. 'Maybe he has changed just as I have changed,' he told himself.

'Interesting man!' commented Snehalatha.

'Oh yes, he is.'

'Did you see those rippling muscles? Like Charles Bronson.'

Marudamuthu called out from outside the room. 'Amma, if you go on chatting it'll soon be dawn.'

'Good night,' said Snehalatha to Kalyanaraman.

'Good night.'

'Please forget what I asked. I meant it as a joke.'

'What did you ask?'

'That means you have forgotten it already. Good,' she remarked and walked out of his room.

Marudamuthu was waiting for her outside. 'Marudamuthu, can you come again tomorrow? I need some help to clear some of the rooms upstairs.'

'Yes, of course I can come,' he replied promptly. Kalyanaraman thought he detected a hint of delight in his voice, apart from the obvious desire to please.

'Ayya,' said Marudamuthu, 'I'll lie down in the verandah. You can sleep peacefully.'

Kalyanaraman was a light sleeper; the slightest sound would wake him. That is what happened later that night. He awoke instantly and listened intently. There was the faintest of sounds … something being moved …

He rose silently and went out of his room without turning on the light. Marudamuthu was fast asleep, huddled under a blanket which was inadequate to muffle his snoring. Next to him on the floor lay a stout stick. Kalyanaraman slid up to him quietly, bent over and tapped the sleeping figure on the shoulder. 'Marudamuthu,' he whispered.

Startled and confused, Marudamuthu sat up with a jerk. 'What … who …?'

Kalyanaraman mimed a warning with a finger against his lips. 'Shhh!' He pointed upwards, mouthing the word '*Mele* … Up.'

Marudamuthu reached under his pillow for a flashlight, rose and picked up his stick. 'Listen first,' urged Kalyanaraman. 'Do you hear any sounds?'

Marudamuthu listened intently. He heard them too. 'You're right, saar. Let's go and see.'

They crept up the stairs as noiselessly as a pair of cats. It was dark upstairs. Marudamuthu's stick hit something in the darkness. Clang! The next moment a series of events happened with lightning speed. Through the hall door that stood open, a dark shadow leapt out and sped towards the balcony. In the blink of an eye it had climbed onto the parapet railing and jumped down onto the roof of the portico below. From there, it was just one more jump down to the ground followed by a sprint into the deep darkness under the trees.

Marudamuthu, in a burst of delayed valour, ran in the direction of the now-invisible intruder. He waved his stick and shouted, 'I'll catch you, I'm going to catch you!'

'What happened?' Kalyanaraman turned. Snehalatha had come upstairs. She had been awakened by Marudamuthu's ruckus.

'We heard sounds from upstairs, so Marudamuthu and I came to investigate. But the fellow ran away before we could catch him.'

Snehalatha stepped fearlessly into the hall, with Kalyanaraman trailing behind her. Their flashlights lit up the whole room. The doors to two of the cupboards stood open. The photograph of the zamindar's wife was hanging crooked on the wall.

'I heard some sounds from upstairs last night too,' Kalyanaraman told her.

She said nothing.

Marudamuthu returned from his futile chase of the mysterious intruder. 'Somehow the fellow slipped away. He must have come to see if he could steal something. Amma, you are awake too. Don't worry, he won't dare to come again. Tonight I somehow drifted off to sleep. From now on I will stay awake at night. Even today if I had reacted an instant earlier I would have caught him. But ayya got scared and let out a scream. I got distracted and the fellow got away.'

'He is lying through his teeth!' fumed Kalyanaraman to Snehalatha. She did not respond. She merely turned and went downstairs in silence. The other two followed.

Snehalatha gave Marudamuthu some instructions. 'Look here, the first thing you need to do in the morning is to find someone to repair the latch of the hall door and buy a big, strong padlock. Tell Thangarasu.'

'All right, ma.'

'Thanks.'

His peaceful sleep having been so rudely disturbed, Kalyanaraman tossed and turned the rest of the night. He fell into a deeper sleep only towards dawn. Strange writhing shadows danced in his dream like modern op art. Then he was chasing a thief through the dense woods. At last the thief came to a stop and said, 'I'm not going to run any longer. Catch me!' Kalyanaraman recoiled in alarm at this strange turn of events.

'Ayya! Ayya!' The shouted words woke him. At the window were the heads of a few young children.

'Who are you?' he asked.

'You asked us to come today, ayya.' A young child among them lisped, 'Give us sweets, ayya!' An older girl hushed him. 'Keep quiet. Of course ayya will give us sweets.'

'All of you form a line and stand quietly. I will come soon,' Kalyanaraman told them. He went to the verandah to look for Marudamuthu, but he was not there. He must have got up early and left for work. Snehalatha's door was shut. He knocked. No response. He tried to open it, but it seemed to be latched on the inside. He went out into the garden and looked through the window. She was fast asleep. The book she had been reading lay open across her chest, and the light in the room was still on. *All right, let her sleep,* he thought.

The children drifted in after him as he went to the wash-house to wash up. They observed him brushing his teeth and washing his face. 'Does he have sweets in his pocket?' a child wondered. Another rubbished that idea. 'No, no, he would have stored them in the house somewhere.'

Having tasted Cadbury's chocolate for the first time in their lives, they were now in his thrall, like the rats that had followed the Pied Piper of Hamelin. It was Kalyanaraman's hope that the lure of chocolates would permit him to teach them to sing harmoniously and render a folk song for him to record.

'What's your name?'

'Karuppayi.'

She was maybe seven years old. She wore only a *pavadai* and no blouse. Her hair which had not seen oil in a long while, was worn in a thin, rat-tail-like plait. On her forehead was the mark of branding with a hot rod, the traditional remedy for indigestion. On her hip, as though permanently attached, sat her little brother.

When they got back to the house, he sent one of the boys on an errand to buy milk. Then he instructed the children once more to stand in line.

'Karuppayi, which is the game you like to play?'

'Hide and seek.'

'All right, now all of you start playing hide and seek. Let me see how you play. Then I will give you all some sweets.'

A period of animated consultation ensued. Who would take on the role of the first seeker seemed to be the point at issue. Karuppayi placed her baby brother aside in a corner. She then walked in front of the line of her friends, tapping each on the shoulder by turn, chanting a line of a song for each:

'*Pacha thavakka palapalakka,*

Pazhani pachan minuminunga

...

Edumbu thudumbu

...

Ettuman kuttuman

... JAL!'

The 'JAL' tap identified the first seeker who would be blindfolded.

'Wait!' said Kalyanaraman. 'Do all of you know this song?'

'Yes, we do.'

'Let me hear you all singing it together.'

'But ... that is not how ...'

'Do you want chocolates or not?'

They sang.

Kalyanaraman tried to get them to harmonize the scale and the notes. After a few attempts he picked out a few with good voices. He told them, 'Now, let's hear it again ... together ... Ettuman, kuttuman ... JAL; Ettuman, kuttuman ... JAL.'

A peal of laughter erupted from somewhere behind him. He whirled around. Snehalatha sat on the steps, hands to her cheeks, laughing in amusement.

'Good morning!' she called out.

'Good morning.'

She rose and approached him. 'Are you going to create a symphony orchestra out of these children?'

'Just give me four days with them and see how they sing. Children, this is enough for today.' He went inside, fetched chocolates and distributed them. The children ran away with their mission for the day accomplished.

'I need to brush my teeth and wash my face,' said Snehalatha. 'Will there be coffee available afterwards?'

'Come, I'll show you the way to the pump house and I'll also make you some coffee.'

They started walking towards the pump house.

'Do you know what tree this is?' asked Snehalatha, pointing to a tree near the path.

'*Ficus religiosa*.'

'Come again?'

'It is the peepul tree, known in Tamil as *arasa maram*. Some of these trees are said to have survived for two thousand years.'

'How do you know so much stuff!' she exclaimed in awe. 'You play the guitar, you are researching folk music, you know so many things … if you go on impressing me like this, I may fall in love with you some day.'

'Really? Please give me a day's notice before that happens,' said Kalyanaraman.

'Why? So that you can run away from here?'

They were now close to the women's bathing spot near the pump house. Kalyanaraman yearned for a glimpse of Velli. *Maybe she will come*, he thought. The sound of anklets from behind them. Velli? He turned.

It was not Velli. Who was this stranger?

6

A MAN. A STRANGER. AN anklet on one leg, flowers behind both ears; mascara magnified his eyes and a felt hat decorated his head. His coat was tight and ill-fitting. He laughed a Chaplinesque laugh. On his shoulder he carried a longish tin box with two lenses embedded at one end. Tucked safely under his armpit was a contraption that appeared to be a kind of easel on a tripod, obviously for setting up the tin box.

'What do you want, ayya?'

'Ayya, my name is Pazhaniandi. I am known even as far as Pandiapuram. They call me "Bioscope Pazhaniandi". I always visit Mempatti during the Visalakshi temple festival. I heard that you pay money to hear music, so I'm here to meet you.'

Snehalatha came up and joined the conversation.

'What's that box?'

'A bioscope, amma. I've stored five concerts, a Haridas performance, MGR, Sivaji Ganesan … everything.'

'Yay!' Snehalatha let out a shriek of excitement. 'I want to see it. Show me, show me!'

'Maybe you should finish brushing your teeth first?' suggested Kalyanaraman.

'What songs do you know?' he asked Pazhaniandi.

Hardly was the question out of Kalyanaraman's mouth than Pazhaniandi launched into song.

'*Come and look, come and look!*
See what I can show you!
The blessed MGR is here,
And the Sivaji of "Parasakthi" fame …'

As he sang, he accompanied himself by beating out the rhythm on the tin box and shaking his leg to make the anklet jingle.

Snehalatha was as excited as a little child. She clapped her hands gleefully and doubled up with laughter.

Kalyanaraman interrupted Pazhaniandi's performance. 'Hey, hey, enough!' he told him. 'That is not a folk song. It's one you made up yourself, isn't it?'

'No, ayya, a man from Mevalapuram wrote it for me.'

'Anyway, it is definitely not a folk song,' proclaimed Kalyanaraman decisively. 'I heard there is a song about the Sivakasi riots. Do you know that one?'

'For that kind of thing, you have to travel south,' Pazhaniandi informed him.

Meanwhile, Snehalatha was peering through the lens of the tin box.

'It's dark in there.'

'Is this amma your wife?' Bioscope Man wanted to know.

'Che, che! She is from the zamindar's family. She is his granddaughter.'

'Is that so? My respects to you, amma.'

'Turn this thing on and show me.'

Kalyanaraman intervened. 'Come back this evening. We can watch the pictures at leisure.'

'Do you have Amitabh Bachchan?' Snehalatha asked eagerly, looking through the photos that were pasted on the bioscope.

'Who's that?' Pazhaniandi was puzzled.

'He won't have anything that dates after 1955,' Kalyanaraman predicted. 'He would just have picked up abandoned bits of cinema reel from here and there …'

'Are you saying that what he sang is not a folk song?'

'That's right, it was not a folk song.'

'So what do you need in a folk song? Should it be one that has never been written down?'

'No, it's not that. If someone from this same district who is unrelated to this man also sings this same song, then it belongs to a folk tradition. Its distinguishing quality is not where it was created but how widely it has spread.'

'If that's your yardstick, then "*Machaanai partheengala*" is also a folk song!' Snehalatha pointed out, mentioning a very popular film song.

'Any song that catches the imagination of a whole society over a time period and speaks to their concerns and lifestyles can become a folk song. For the "*Machaan*" song you mentioned, it's still too early to judge. If it is still sung in common people's homes fifteen years from now, then we can call it a "folk song".'

'You argue very well.'

'I'm only talking about what I've read and studied,' he said, careful not to meet her gaze.

Marudamuthu was coming towards them, along with Velli and another woman.

Kalyanaraman brightened visibly at the sight of Velli; he also realized that Snehalatha had sensed his reaction.

'Oh, so you are here,' remarked Marudamuthu. 'I went and looked in the house first ...'

'This is Velli,' said Kalyanaraman, making the introduction. The two women looked at each other in silence for a while, as though sizing each other up. 'Hello, sweet girl!' said Snehalatha.

Meanwhile, Marudamuthu was shouting at Bioscope Man. 'Ey! So you've turned up here also, eh? Get lost! Take your box and run away.' He accompanied his abuse with a blow from his stick.

'Wait, wait!' protested Kalyanaraman. 'Why are you hitting him?'

'Ayya, you don't know ... you must never trust these kinds of people ... GO! Didn't you hear me, GO NOW!'

Bioscope Man hurriedly picked up his tin box and fled in sheer terror, the tinkle of his anklet fading into the distance. It seemed to Kalyanaraman that Marudamuthu's treatment of the man was totally unwarranted. Maybe he just wanted to parade his idea of valour to Snehalatha.

All the while, Velli had been staring fixedly at Snehalatha. Kalyanaraman looked at the two women, and the photographer in him was struck by the contrasts in the freeze frame: Sungadi sari … man's shirt; dark complexion … fair-skinned. If only he could take a photograph there and then! A caption popped up in his mind: 'A Study in Contrasts'.

'Did you sleep well?' Marudamuthu asked Snehalatha in a friendly tone.

'Yes, I did, Marudamuthu.'

'Coffee and breakfast?'

'Not yet. I want to wash up and have a bath first.'

'Have you arranged for hot water?' Marudamuthu asked Velli.

Silence. She had been gazing back and forth between Marudamuthu and Snehalatha during their exchange.

'Velli! Have you stuffed chalk in your ears or what …?'

'What?'

'Have you arranged for hot water?'

'Where?'

'I told you yesterday!'

'You didn't tell me anything.'

'Wait and see what I do … are you trying to play a joke?'

'It's all right,' said Snehalatha. 'I'll try a cold water bath. Velli, will you take me to the bathing place, please?'

Velli looked at Marudamuthu. He, meantime, was gazing at Snehalatha.

'I will take you there,' he offered.

'Ayye, che! How will you come into the place where women are bathing? *Ennadi*, why is this man showing so much concern for me?'

'Amma, it is because you are from the zamin family,' Marudamuthu explained. 'I will step aside while you have your bath, and when you have finished …'

Kalyanaraman sorted out the situation. 'Let them both go and finish their baths, Marudamuthu. We will wait here for them.'

Velli led the way with Snehalatha following.

'The revenue officer in the town wants to meet you,' Marudamuthu informed Kalyanaraman.'

'Is that so?'

'And I told Thangarasu about the fellow who sneaked in last night. It's not safe for amma to be alone. I will come here every night.'

'All right.'

'Ayya, I heard you are going to move to the town ...?'

'No. Who told you that?'

'What will Snehamma do for food?'

So Snehalatha had now become 'Snehamma'!

'I don't know.'

A sudden loud shriek from Snehalatha sent Marudamuthu sprinting to find out what was wrong. He soon returned looking sheepish. The first feel of the cold water on her bare skin had made the lady yell in shock. But it was all good; she was actually enjoying it.

Marudamuthu's gaze kept returning often to the direction from which Snehalatha would return after her bath.

When Snehalatha returned, she was limping slightly. Velli and the other woman followed a little further behind.

'What happened to your leg, amma?' asked Marudamuthu in a voice full of concern.

'She stepped in cow dung,' explained Velli, laughing.

'Don't just stand there. Pour water for her to wash her foot,' he ordered.

'Yes, yes! I will wash her feet,' retorted Velli and poured water on Snehalatha's foot.

'So I'll get going, Marudamuthu,' said Snehalatha, preparing to return to the house.

'I'll walk back with you,' he offered. 'Velli, you can leave now.'

Kalyanaraman walked ahead while Marudamuthu engaged Snehalatha in conversation a few steps behind. Kalyanaraman was sure there was more to Marudamuthu's interest in Snehalatha than the fact that she was from the family of a rich former employer. He was also sure that Velli would have sensed that as well.

When they reached the house, Snehalatha said, 'Thanks, Marudamuthu.'

'When shall I come again?'

'What for?'

'You said you would teach me English.'

'Did I say that?'

'Yes, you did, amma.'

'This ayya here will be a very good teacher. He is highly qualified. Get hold of him for your English tuition.'

'No, no, I prefer to have you teach me. You speak English better and more correctly.'

'All right, come tomorrow.'

'Your shirt is wet, amma. Please go and change it. If you want me to bring anything from the town, let me know. I will come back tonight anyway.'

'All right.'

Marudamuthu left, rather reluctantly.

'Nice fellow!' remarked Snehalatha. 'See how innocent these village fellows are.'

Kalyanaraman had half a mind to tell her, 'He is not as innocent as you think.' But he restrained himself.

'That Velli of yours doesn't speak at all,' Snehalatha remarked as she entered her room.

Kalyanaraman busied himself. He boiled milk, poured it into two cups, added instant coffee and sugar, stirred well and carried the cups across to Snehalatha's room.

'Ma'am, coffee is ready!'

Snehalatha came out of her room. Kalyanaraman was looking down at the cups in his hand. 'It's only instant coffee … it will be just average …' he started to say, looking up … and the words died on his lips. She was in a thin white *jibba* with nothing under it. Her nipples were faintly visible against the cloth.

'What are you staring at?'

Kalyanaraman managed to recover his poise. He swallowed and said, 'It's not a good idea to dress like this in the village. You had better wear something under it.'

'But no one will come here now. We are free.'

'As you wish.'

'The coffee is good. You do everything well. Tell me, what else can you do?'

Kalyanaraman looked out through the window.

'Please go into your room, please …' he urged her, the sense of urgency plain in his voice.

'Why?'

'Some elderly visitor is coming towards the front door, and it won't look good if …'

'Okay, okay.' She disappeared into her room and shut the door.

Thangarasu had brought a visitor.

'Welcome, Thangarasu.'

'This gentleman is Ayyadurai. He is the revenue official.'

'Is that so? Namaskaram!'

There was a large mole on Ayyadurai's face. On his forehead was a big sandal-paste pottu. His nose was like a capsicum, and several of his teeth seemed to be missing. He was not wearing an upper garment, and the thick white fuzz on his chest reminded Kalyanaraman of pictures of Russian bear cubs.

'Thangarasu, last night again we heard movement from upstairs,' said Kalyanaraman.

'Yes, Muthu told me. I heard he ran away? Ayyadurai saar, thieves are roaming around …'

'Who's the fellow? Tell me. I will chop off his legs.'

'The day before yesterday I found cigarette stubs on the terrace. An expensive brand.'

'Oh, that! That's nothing to worry about. Last month the collector visited and wanted to look around the building. He went up to the terrace too. He was smoking cigarettes. This other matter has nothing to do with that. This is the work of some thieving rascals. Anyway, I'll make sure the hall door is repaired and properly locked.'

'I heard the zamindar's granddaughter is here?' asked Ayyadurai.

'Yes, she is in her room. Snehalatha!' Kalyanaraman called out.

'This ayya … remember I told you the PDA had written to me? He is the visitor who has come to collect folk songs.'

'Oh … that's good! Thangarasu, did you spot that *neerkatti* fellow … the one with the large boil? He's missing for fifteen days now. Maybe he overdosed on *kungiliyam* and is lying senseless somewhere.'

'Ponnusamy has found himself a woman in the town.'

Snehalatha emerged from her room, cutting short the gossip session. She had taken Kalyanaraman's advice. She now wore a Nehru jacket over the thin jibba.

'Here she is!' announced Thangarasu.

'Come closer, child,' invited Ayyadurai. He looked at her intently. With cataracts in both eyes drawing a thin veil over his vision, he stepped even closer to inspect her. He reached out and touched her. His old, yellowed eyes brimmed with tears. 'She is the exact replica of Ratnavathy Amma!' he quavered.

Snehalatha smiled. 'Oh, do you know all those people?'

'The child is asking if I know them …!' laughed Ayyadurai. 'My child, your grandfather bought a horse in Madurai and had golden horseshoes fitted on him. He was very wealthy. He bought an English book worth ten pauns of gold in those days. He could pluck flowers from the sky … He left so much money even to his concubine … enough to construct two large community halls.'

'A … hem …' Thangarasu cleared his throat to stop the awkward flow of words from the old man.

'Sweet!' declared Snehalatha, with a conspiratorial wink to Kalyanaraman.

The old man coughed. Thangarasu hurriedly steered the conversation onto safer paths. 'This Maniyarar grew up in your ancestral home, amma.'

'Oh, really? That's great! Thatha, please sit down and rest. You are coughing.'

'Look, she called me "thatha". Please ask me for whatever you want, child. Eight generations of my family owe allegiance to yours.'

Thangarasu whispered an aside to Kalyanaraman. 'The people around him brought about his ruin.'

'Ayyadurai saar, let's go. It's getting late. You can talk later. I have to get to the fields. Pichaipillai has been raising a ruckus about a water issue.'

'My dear child, I will have to go now …'

'All right, thatha.'

'And you, young man, if you are looking for songs, just ask me. "*Marudai Veeran*", "*Alli Arasani*" …' said Ayyadurai, garbling names cheerfully.

'All right, saar.'

After they were out of earshot, Snehalatha remarked, 'What strange people!' She squirmed a bit and said, 'It's so sweaty, isn't it?' She proceeded to take off her Nehru jacket.

Kalyanaraman turned and retreated into his room.

In a short while, a loud, high-pitched scream rent the air. It came from Snehalatha's room …

7

THE MOMENT HE HEARD Snehalatha screaming, Kalyanaraman ran to her room. The door was open. She was cowering near the bed, looking terrified. 'There! There!' she squealed, pointing towards a wooden cupboard. 'Some dark fellow. Horrible face!'

In a state of great agitation, Kalyanaraman approached the cupboard. He stamped his foot on the ground a couple of times as a warning and called out, 'Ey! Who's there? Come out!'

Snehalatha ran up from behind Kalyanaraman and embraced him. He felt himself enveloped in her warmth. She pointed to the opposite corner. 'There! There!'

Kalyanaraman wheeled around in alarm. She burst out laughing. 'It was a joke.'

Kalyanaraman extricated himself from her embrace. He was very embarrassed indeed. Actually, that was the very first time he had ever been in such close physical contact with a woman.

'Don't ever play this kind of joke again. Otherwise, even if there is a real need, I won't come.'

'Take it easy, yaar,' she said, laughing heartily once more. 'Kalyanaraman, you have disappointed me. You're no good! You didn't take this opportunity to grab me, hold me close and plant a kiss on my …'

Kalyanaraman interrupted her. 'I'm not that kind of man.'

'What if it was Velli instead of me?' she teased, and winked at him.

'Don't be silly!' he protested sternly. He didn't know how to label her behaviour. Childishness? Jealousy? Or just teasing and horseplay?

'Come on, Raman, your eyes give you away. When you look at Velli, they widen like saucers. Now don't bluff … tell me, don't you have a crush on Velli?'

'You have not understood me properly. My interest is only in folk music.'

'It will start with folk music and then go to sweet girls who sing folk music. Be careful! Have you noticed that Marudamuthu is built like a wrestler?'

'Enough of this childish talk!' Kalyanaraman walked out in a state of high irritation. She had invaded a private space in his mind, one that he had been attempting to safeguard. *I have to be careful*, he told himself. *What if she blabbers something like this to Marudamuthu?* Momentarily he visualized himself engaged in a tussle with Marudamuthu in a field somewhere …

He walked slowly towards the village. The children who had come to the house earlier spotted him. 'Chocolate Dorai, Chocolate Dorai!' they chanted. Young Karuppayi grabbed the hand of the little brother who was attached to her hip as usual and held it out towards Kalyanaraman. In a kind of reflex action the little boy turned his palm upwards, the universal gesture for 'Give me'.

He wondered whether he should give them some money. But then he decided against it. They would swarm around and pester him. He chased them all away. They scattered but kept watch from a distance.

At the entrance to the temple, under the shade of a tree, Bioscope Man was fast asleep. His loud snores indicated he was lost to the world. The equipment that gave him his livelihood stood near him, covered with a cloth.

Inside the temple, four roughly hewn stone pillars supported an asbestos roof. The words 'Ponnammal Donations' were picked out in neon lights. In the tiny room, the goddess Amman stood backed up against the wall. Her eyes were wide. She wore a red sari with a gold-thread border and false jewellery in the traditional style. Tiny toy cradles hung from the ceiling, and little wisps and knots of thread lay as offerings to Amman from devotees seeking Her blessings.

The pujari's house was nearby but separate from the temple. His wife was nursing their latest child at her breast. The other children and a few hens were running around in the sun. Kalyanaraman walked around the temple. A thorny pathway, a disused well with a variety of living creatures flourishing on the green, oily scum on the surface of the water, a stone platform.

'It will surely happen in the month of Thai, amma. Bring a sari for Amman. On the first of the month, have a bath at home and come to the temple in wet clothes. Bring a chicken with you.'

'I will do so, pujari.'

Velli was sitting on the floor facing the pujari. She accepted his offering of kumkumam reverentially and applied it on her forehead. 'It is Amman's blessing. Now … a rupee.' He held out a hand.

Velli undid eight knots in her sari pallu, extracted a note and handed it to the pujari. She noticed Kalyanaraman and rose to her feet.

The pujari turned. 'Oh, is he the one?' he asked Velli. *She has told him about me*, thought Kalyanaraman. Velli was silent.

'My greetings, ayya,' said the pujari.

'What, Velli, are you getting your future foretold?'

She looked embarrassed.

Kalyanaraman turned towards the pujari.

'Pujari Ayya, do you know any songs?'

'I sing only when the Sami is taken in a procession,' the pujari informed him. Kalyanaraman took a close look at the man. An untidy ritual tuft of hair at the back of his head, a hatchet-shaped moustache, a bracelet on his arm and several metal rings on various fingers. 'Then too, I am not the one singing. Sami sings through me.' He laughed through missing teeth.

'The next time the Sami is going to be taken in a procession will you send word to me?'

'But how is that . . .?' The pujari rubbed his bare chest. *Could do with a bra*, thought Kalyanaraman.

'I will pay you, Pujari Ayya.'

'All right, I will send word, saar.'

Velli had moved away and was chatting with the pujari's wife.

'The whole village is talking about that new woman. They say she wears a shirt like a man and is up to all kinds of behaviour.'

'True, Thangamma. She's turned up like some loose woman . . .'

'Anyway, get back safe before dark. A thief is loose in the night.'

Spotting Kalyanaraman, the woman asked in a feeble voice, 'Who's this?'

'This gentleman is also staying in the zamin house. He has come from Madras. He wants to listen to our music.'

'What is that Marudamuthu fellow up to these days?'

'That woman stepped in some cow dung, and he tells me to wash her feet for her! He wants her to teach him English. The whole thing doesn't look good at all, Thangamma! Anyway, I have to go now. I'll see you later. Pujari Ayya, I'm leaving.'

Velli walked in silence, and Kalyanaraman followed a few steps behind her. The dog, Mani, which had been waiting for Velli at the temple gate, joined her, tail wagging in joy.

In the distance was a dense thicket of trees.

'Come, Velli, let us go away by ourselves into that grove of trees. No one will see us there.'

'Yes, I will come, I will come,' said Velli.

The sound of a cycle bell disturbed this delightful scene that had been playing in Kalyanaraman's mind. He stepped aside. It was Marudamuthu on the cycle. Comfortably perched behind him on the carrier was Snehalatha, as carefree as though sitting on a park swing.

'Ayya, good morning! Good night! Velli, tomorrow I'm taking Snehamma to the town. We will go along the lakeside. We're going to buy books.'

'Hi, Kalyanaraman! Hi, Velli!' called out Snehalatha. As the cycle snaked away into the far distance towards the clump of trees, Snehalatha looked back and laughed till they were lost to view.

Velli stood stunned. *What has got into that man!* she thought to herself.

Kalyanaraman seemed to have read her mind. 'He's just happy that the zamin family amma is here, that's all.'

'No, saar. Since yesterday he has been acting strange. He keeps mentioning "Snehamma" in every sentence. After asking the workers to come to the fields he is taking joyrides on his cycle!'

'He will come back.'

'If my father sees this, what will he think? That woman doesn't seem to understand what modesty means! Che!'

'Velli, will you fetch Periatha?'

'When is she planning to leave?'

'Who?'

'Who else? That mannish butterfly.'

'She mentioned that she plans to stay here for about a week ...'

'Oh God!' Velli bit on a bead from her necklace in frustration. Her eyes conveyed her distress, although the kumkumam on her forehead, applied with the blessings of the pujari, signified hope that the month of Thai would bring good tidings ...

She became aware that Kalyanaraman had his eyes fixed on her. She adjusted her sari across her chest and said, 'I'll go home.'

'Will you bring Periatha?'

'I will send her,' she replied over her shoulder.

Kalyanaraman blurted out, 'Velli, if you come I will teach you English.'

She stopped, turned and looked at him. 'That sort of thing is beyond me, saar. I am destined to be illiterate. I've never held a slate. I've never seen the inside of a school. Ever since I can remember, whatever I have learnt has been from that man. And now he is rushing away … running from me …'

She moved away, talking softly to herself. Kalyanaraman went back to the zamin house. Periatha was waiting there for him even without being reminded. She welcomed him with a wide smile, lips and teeth stained red with betel juice. 'Saar, you are a prince. With the money you gave me I wanted to buy a pretty waistband for my granddaughter … but that wretched woman my son has married, she is pregnant again. So I just bought a lot of sweets … all the money you gave me is over.' She emphasized the point by holding out her empty palms.

'Wait a minute.' Kalyanaraman went indoors. He looked for his cigarette packet but couldn't find it. Maybe he had dropped it in Snehalatha's room when he rushed there earlier. He went over to her door. It was locked. He looked through the window. Wait … what was all this?

The photograph of Ratnavathy Amma, the zamindar's wife, had mysteriously made its way from the upstairs hall to Snehalatha's room and now stood against a wall. Nearby, a lot of old books lay scattered.

He went to where Periatha was waiting. 'How are you, Periatha?'

'I'm all right thanks to your large heart.'

'Did you know Ratnavathy Amma?'

'Yes, I knew her very well. Why do you ask?'

'Nothing, just curious.'

'She lives in this house.'

'What do you mean?'

'After she died she has been roaming around this place. Once when my son was a child he saw her near the tamarind tree. He was so terrified he soiled his pants.'

Kalyanaraman laughed. 'Oh, all right!'

'You're laughing! People like you who come from Madras don't believe these things ...'

'When did she die?'

'About forty years ago. In the month of Aipasi.'

'What did she die of? Did she catch a disease?'

'Disease?' Periatha prepared another mouthful of betel leaf in a leisurely manner before picking up the thread of the conversation. 'Not a disease. *Maandukittu poyitaga*.'

'Maandukittu ...? What does that mean?'

'She hanged herself. I saw that scene with my own eyes. I must have been sixteen or so at the time. Her hair was wild, her kumkumam was smeared, she had cast away all her ornaments. She was hanging from a stout rope tied to a hook in the ceiling that was meant to hold a swing. But her face was peaceful. Ayya was taking a stroll in the garden. Such a commotion broke loose! Lots of people came crowding. The police came to take down her body. Then a hearse was arranged from Thirunilam ... you can't imagine ...

If a woman weeps and relates her woes
Under a mango tree;
Even the peacock that sits atop that tree
Will forgo its food in sympathy ...'

Kalyanaraman interrupted her song hastily. 'Why did she hang herself?'

'She was very unhappy. Ayya had a roving eye. He had many mistresses, White women too. Drinks would flow freely ... red drinks, green drinks. If he saw any reasonably attractive woman anywhere, he would order that she should be sent to him. It happened to me once. I was there for a chore. "Are you here to pound rice?" he asked, and grabbed my hand. I dropped the pestle on the floor, freed myself and fled. The way he looked at women was disgusting. Seeking pleasure all the time. What was that poor amma to do? What's the use of having tonnes of jewellery and riding in a grand horse chariot if there is no happiness? She was illiterate. He forced her to take tuition at home from White women teachers. He insisted that she should learn to speak English. He forced her to drink liquor. Poor voiceless creature ... she was comfortable only with temple festivals and traditional games like *pallankuzhi* and *dayakattai* ... that was her world. But he forced her to try to learn so many unfamiliar things. It is said he even horse-whipped her to make her obey him.'

During Periatha's calm narration of these events, Kalyanaraman's mind painted a vivid image of the scene.

The hall, with a chandelier suspended from the centre of the ceiling; in the corner the gramophone with the picture of a dog is playing a waltz. The zamindar, 'May it please Your Excellency', the lord and master, is presiding over his domain. The tinkling of glasses being passed around; on the blood-red carpet, the swish-swish of pirouetting, swan-like dancers; ghazal singers in attendance, women from the north in their fine muslins. And liquor ... liquor ...

In the room next door, Ratnavathy sits reciting 'C ... a ... t ... CAT ... M ... a ... t ... MAT. Mary had a little lamb' to the accompaniment of sounds of merriment from the hall ... laughter, coy protests and dance music.

Then, in his muslin jibba, eyes red from drinking and hair in a tangle, reeking of cigarettes and liquor, the zamindar enters her room. In his hand, a whip. He winds the thong carefully over the handle.

'Don't beat me! Don't whip me! I will learn. I will sing. I will talk.'

Periatha was approaching the end of her reminiscences. 'She was so fond of jewellery, that lady. But in the end she threw it all away before she killed herself. I can see her clearly to this day. She looked like a doll. Chubby cheeks, a kumkumam pottu the size of a quarter-anna coin on her forehead. She would go every day in the chariot to the Amman temple. Whenever she saw me on the way, she would stop and make enquiries. "How are you?" she would ask, "How are you doing?" and she would gift me some money.'

Kalyanaraman looked through the window again at the picture of Ratnavathy. Decked in mounds of jewellery but with sheer terror in those eyes, as though someone had draped the ornaments on her and ordered her to stand still for a photo. 'Ayya, can you spare a rupee? I need some betelnut and a measure of rice.'

'And also you favourite malli coffee, right?'

'Do you want to listen to my songs?'

'No, Periatha, I'm not in the mood right now.'

'Huh?'

'Mm ... how many children did the lady have?'

'She would tearfully beg of her two grown sons, "Will you two at least save me from misery?"'

'What about her parents?'

'That was another family that ruined itself. If this zamindar blindly leapt eight feet, that one leaped sixteen! He went to Bombay, invested his money in films and lost it all. That's why Ratnavathy Amma has never once stepped foot outside this village after she got married. That's why she is still hovering around here. Once the wind and rain of Aipasi are over she makes her appearance without fail every year.'

'Have you seen her?'

'My son has seen her. So has that *neerkatti* boy ... you know, the fellow with the big cyst.'

'It's all a hoax.'

'Look at that tamarind tree. Do you see even a blade of grass growing in its shade? Look at the shade under all the other trees. If a ghost lives in a tree, nothing will grow under it.'

'All tamarind trees are like this,' he wanted to explain. 'It's because of the acidic vapours that they put out.' But how could he get that idea across to this old woman who was hard of hearing to start with? He decided to let it go.

'Right, you should get back now, Periatha.'

'Don't wander around outside after dark,' she warned him.

'All right,' he said, and laughed.

He cooked a modest meal for himself and after he had eaten he took a nap. The village children arrived and he managed to get them to sing a song reasonably well by offering chocolates as incentives.

Dusk was approaching, and still no sign of Snehalatha. Finally, it was Velli who appeared.

8

VELLI WAS ACCOMPANIED BY a small boy and the ever-faithful dog Mani. She stopped at the front door, swishing a neem sprig back and forth. As Kalyanaraman hurriedly put on a shirt and stepped out of his room she asked, 'They're not back yet?'

'No …'

'It's almost dark. There's been no word from him since he left with her this morning. The workers waited for a long time in the fields and then went away to some other job.' Velli talked feverishly without meeting Kalyanaraman's eyes in a voice choked with anxiety. Her body language both attracted Kalyanaraman and distracted him from what she was saying.

'They will come,' he said soothingly.

'But what was he up to the whole day?'

'I've no idea.'

'That woman is no good, saar …'

'Akka, a goat kid is missing. Shall I go and look for it?' the little boy wanted to know.

'Wait, da. Saar, he never stays out so late. He always gets back before dark. Perhaps he plans to stay out the whole night. That woman has deliberately lured him …'

'Akka, you said this ayya will give me chocolates,' put in the boy hopefully.

'Maybe they have gone to a cinema show,' suggested Kalyanaraman.

Velli flared up in fury. 'How dare you go to a cinema! How dare you go without me, ya? Won't the serpents of hell attack you?'

'Whom are you talking to, Velli?'

'To him! That man! He's a good man, ayya. Last year he was lured by two fellows in fine mull dhotis. He followed them and they took him somewhere far away. He got scared and ran back. He is not sly or dishonest, ayya. He is not capable of scheming.'

'Why are you so tense about it? They will return soon.'

'Akka ... AKKA ... chocolate!'

'Please give this little monkey a chocolate, ayya. He is such a pest.'

'What's your name?'

'Rajavelu.'

'All right, I'm giving you eight annas. Run and buy sweets for yourself and your akka here.'

The little fellow switched on an imaginary tractor engine. 'Vrrr ... Vrrr.' He engaged gear and drove off at full speed, whooping as he went. '*Kuchi kuchi Rakkamma, koosana Rakkamma.*'

Daylight was rapidly fading. 'Sit down, Velli,' he invited. She chewed nervously at the neem twig and her gaze was riveted on the gate. When she sat down the rays of the setting sun bathed her in a pale glow. She was a statue carved in gold. As he stood in front of her, he could see the cleavage of her breasts. The plastic bead necklace nestled inside ... Kalyanaraman suddenly felt feverish.

He grabbed her, pushed her flat on the floor and started undoing her clothes. All in his imagination.

'Velli, give me your hand. I know how to read palms.'

After some initial hesitation she held out one hand. He didn't quite have the courage to reach out and hold her hand. Instead he moved closer to inspect her upturned palm. He gently traced one of the lines with his little finger. In a very natural reaction she withdrew her hand, handed him the neem twig and said, 'Use this.'

'The light is too dim out here. Why don't you come inside?' He turned on the light in his room. She stepped inside rather reluctantly. His eyes moved to her midriff and admired how her sari was tucked at her waist.

'Sit,' he instructed. She sat on the floor.

'You want your deepest wish to come true, right?'

'Yes, yes, saar.'

'What is your deepest wish?'

'He should not change. He should always be the same as he was. I'm tortured with worry about him ...'

'Pooh! Is that all! Repeat after me: "Om Nama Sivaya!"'

'Om Nama Sivaya.'

'Om, Om! Shut your eyes, otherwise the magic won't work.'

She shut her eyes. He went up close to her; he held his face near hers. The scent of neem oil; the scent of the earth; the scent of wet fields of grain; the scent of beauty. With his fingertips he held the fold of the sari that covered her breasts. His heart jumped into his throat. Gently he put his arms around her and held her in an embrace. She recoiled and shuddered. Her eyes flew open. She pushed him away. He caught her hand.

'Leave me alone! Leave me!' she pleaded. Glass bangles shattered. He pulled her towards him. With a strength born of desperation she freed herself. Then, holding the pallu of her sari against her mouth for comfort, she said, 'Che! You are an educated man. A big man from a big city. This is not good. If he hears about this he will take a sickle to you.'

'Sorry, sorry,' muttered Kalyanaraman weakly. He was trembling.

'Drrr ... Vrrr ...' Rajavelu's imaginary tractor was roaring in, to the usual accompaniment of '*Kuchi kuchi Rakkamma*.'

'Here are your sweets, akka.'

She took the packet from the child and placed it on the table. 'I'll go now, saar. If he comes, don't tell him Velli waited here for him.'

'But why are you leaving the sweets for me?'

'Come along, you little monkey, I'll buy you other sweets. We won't take these. Idiot that I am, I must have set out at an inauspicious hour. And I trimmed my nails on a Tuesday. Wretched, wretched me!'

Kalyanaraman sighed deeply. He felt a distinct sense of relief. He stood watching the departing figures and thought to himself, *How can I communicate with these people? I went and forced myself on a woman who is obviously in love with her Marudamuthu. What an idiotic thing I've done! It was wrong of me to lust for her from the very beginning. What if she tells Marudamuthu?* A spasm of fear ran through him. She was an innocent young woman. She might go and describe the whole thing to Marudamuthu. *No, no, she won't. She will keep it to herself. This time she won't tell. Don't repeat this, ever*, he admonished himself.

He changed into a lungi and went and lay down. In his imagination he turned into a Walter Mitty and rescued Velli from dire danger. He battled his way through floodwaters to rescue that fellow Rajavelu, bring him ashore and wring him dry. He saved Velli from a savage wild boar by spearing it to death till it lay in a bloody heap. And what about Marudamuthu? He hung lifeless from the branch of a tree ...

'No, no!'

He rose at the sound of a cycle bell. Two figures loomed out of the darkness as the bicycle approached closer. Snehalatha was in front, seated on the crossbar.

'Hi, Ram!'

Marudamuthu cycled right up to where Kalyanaraman stood and brought the cycle to a sudden stop with a dramatic screeching of brakes.

'Oh, what a lovely ride!' declared Snehalatha.

'Why so late?'

'We went to a cinema. What was the name, Marudamuthu?' Her hair was in disarray.

'*Jaganmohini.*'

'Sex, bhakthi ... good combination. Marudamuthu was so attentive ... so attentive ... *adada!*'

'Did Velli come here for me?' he asked, his voice guilt-laden.

Kalyanaraman could not tell a lie. 'Yes, she waited here for you a long time.'

'And were you watching her all the time?' asked Snehalatha slyly.

'Velli has no other job. Once every hour she will look for me,' remarked Marudamuthu.

'Look after her carefully, Marudamuthu. There are birds of prey here that might pluck her away,' suggested Snehalatha.

Kalyanaraman glared at her.

'This fellow must be good in bed,' she said in English and laughed, indicating Marudamuthu.

Kalyanaraman stared at her aghast.

'You're saying something in English. Snehamma, someday I will also learn English and I will be able to say, "This fellow vish bishavish ..."'

She applauded and laughed in delight. Encouraged by her reaction, he amused her with a couple of more minutes of his manufactured 'English'. Snehalatha laughed till tears streamed down her face. She reached into her bag, took out a small bottle of perfume and sprayed it on Marudamuthu's face. Bathed in a cloud of perfume, Marudamuthu wriggled and squirmed in a parody of Jaganmohini's dance in the cinema. More applause and laughter from Snehalatha. Grim, stony silence from Kalyanaraman.

'I'll leave now, saar. I'll come back to sleep.' With a sidelong glance at Snehalatha, Marudamuthu held the side of the cycle seat, leapt on gracefully and cycled away with much tinkling of the bell.

'You are teasing him. Toying with him. You're making an idiot of him.'

'Jealous?'

'Che! Don't imagine things! Anyway, I've been wanting to ask you … I saw Ratnavathy Amma's photo in your room. Why did you take it down from the wall upstairs and bring it to your room?'

She seemed a bit uncomfortable with the question but managed it well. 'I thought I would take it back with me. Anyway I wanted to use Marudamuthu's help to clear out the upstairs hall. I want to tear up all those old papers. Here, I thought you might be hungry. I brought you fruit bread.'

'Thanks.'

'Just "thanks"?'

'If that's not enough, I can play a song for you on my guitar.'

'That's all? Very, very bad!' She went into her room but emerged a while later, asking, 'Kalyanaraman, do you happen to have a safety pin?'

He looked at her disdainfully. 'Look, I know you have a lot of other shirts and garments, all with buttons. Why pick the one that needs a pin?'

'You don't like me, Raman.'

'I think you're trying to make a fool of me like you are doing with Marudamuthu. The poor fellow will be going to Velli reeking of the perfume you sprayed on him.'

She laughed.

Does the woman have no sense of decency? Is this something to laugh about? he seethed inwardly.

'What did you do to her?'

'To whom?'

'To Velli. You may have lured her into your room. "Come, I will show you a trick … I will play a song for you" … take her into the dark room …'

'Che!' There was a book in his hand. He flung it at her in fury. She caught it neatly and looked at the title. *Leela Tilakam*. She opened the first page.

Paalodu thulya …

She snapped it shut and tossed it back to him briskly. 'I have a book. Do you want to see it?'

'What is it? *Playboy* magazine?'

'No, *Playgirl*. Goodnight, *tambura*!' She pouted. 'Not enough gumption, ayyare. Too ho-hum. You need to eat some *lehiam* to cure you.'

As Kalyanaraman lay in his room in the dark, the thought of her antics brought a smile to his lips. In the silence of the night he thought to himself, *What a woman*! He couldn't get to sleep. He sat up, picked up his guitar and started strumming a classical number. 'Shut u … u … U … UP!' shouted Snehalatha from her room. Marudamuthu was fast asleep on the verandah. He could just walk to her room, knock on the door and ask, 'Snehalatha, how about it?'

No, NO, NO. It's wrong. Mm … hmm. Sleep, sleep …

The tractor stands silent. Kalyanaraman, Marudamuthu, Velli and Snehalatha run frantically round and round the tractor. Ratnavathy and Periatha stand to one side urging them on. 'Faster! Faster!' Ratnavathy cracks her whip. 'If you stop, your dhoti will fall off!' warns Periatha. Then Ratnavathy is hanging with a rope around her neck.

'How does it feel?' he asks her.

'It's painful at first, but you gradually get used to it. The real nuisance is the way my legs are twitching. That, and I want to urinate …'

Yes, he wanted to urinate. Outside, the moon was high in the sky and the whole world was bathed in its glow. Kalyanaraman stepped out onto the verandah and proceeded to empty his bladder into the garden in full view of anyone who happened to be watching. From the spreading branches of the tamarind tree, an owl hooted. With tiny sounds accompanying it, the tree rustled gently in the breeze.

Ratna! The woman who had suffered whiplashes, the woman who had hanged herself. In the middle of the night she was calling him. 'Come, I will tell you my story. Come along, ayya. You can hear about how I lost everything ...

In Thiruchendur, the temple chariot is bedecked,
Flowers adorn the hair of the courtesan.
In the morning he wears a kambi dhoti
In the afternoon, he wears mull;
In the evening his dhoti has gold thread;
At dusk, there are concubines.
Oh, dishonourable schemer,
Oh, worshipper of rain,
You brought your concubines,
And invited ruin on the land.'

Ratnavathy sang. She laughed. Was her voice echoing from the tamarind tree? Or was it resonating inside his mind?

Kalyanaraman stepped cautiously closer to the tree. Now a waltz tune could be heard playing. A big party was going on in the zamindar's hall. All kinds of sounds. He went even closer. And now the sound of footsteps ...

Ratnavathy's voice? Nonsense!!

It must be the same intruder who had been visiting every night. The sounds were not coming from the tamarind tree at all. Sounds of people moving around. Footsteps. The branches of the tree brushed the parapet wall of the upper verandah. A figure leapt silently from the parapet onto a branch of the tree and started climbing down.

In a sudden burst of daring, Kalyanaraman stepped silently towards the foot of the tree and awaited the arrival of the intruder. He clutched his chest to still the thumping of his heart. The nimble intruder slid down the tree trunk.

Kalyanaraman jumped upon the unsuspecting man, shouting loudly at the same time, 'Marudamuthu!' The two wrapped their arms around each other like lovers as they wrestled in the mud. Kalyanaraman became aware of the man's sweat, the warmth of his body, the smell of his flesh … Suddenly, he felt a sharp, stabbing pain in his side. He loosened his grasp. Then … a blow to the head. Unaware he had been hit, unaware of what had hit him, he tried to call out, 'Marudamuthu! Marudamuthu!' The words died to a whisper on his lips. He fell unconscious.

9

WHEN KALYANARAMAN REGAINED CONSCIOUSNESS and opened his eyes he was confronted by Snehalatha's smiling face.

'So you're alive!'

His shoulders hurt. His head throbbed. His whole body ached. He couldn't get up off the ground.

'They're saying you were attacked by a spirit. I'm told my grandmother inhabits this tree as a ghost.'

'No, no,' he protested weakly. 'There was a man … a fellow … he came down …'

'When did you see a strange fellow? Yesterday? The day before?' Snehalatha was sceptical.

The ever-valorous Marudamuthu was also at the scene now. 'If you had woken me, we could have caught him on the spot, tied him to the tree and flayed him alive. Snehamma, it's dangerous for you to be in this house. It's better for you to move closer to where I live.'

'Nonsense! I'm not scared of things like this.'

'Ayya can move away to the town …'

'Ayya can't move at all right now,' remarked Snehalatha. 'Here, take these,' she said, handing Kalyanaraman some pills. 'Why do you take on this kind of fight when you are not up to it?'

Kalyanaraman could express his annoyance only with his eyes. He looked around. Ayyadurai was there. Snehalatha, Marudamuthu … *adede*, there was Velli in the corner. Thangarasu had also come, and there was one other man, a stranger.

The stranger spoke. 'This man you saw … can you describe him?'

'Who are you?'

'I'm the outpost constable, sir.'

A constable? This man? Khaki shirt and dhoti, blue bag … and an enormous moustache even larger than his face. Slim build …

'Periasamy, you should inform the inspector,' suggested Thangarasu. 'This fellow has been sneaking around here the past three nights. He must be a stranger to the village.'

'Have they filed a complaint?'

'We will ask ayya here to give a statement. I will send a report to the inspector and to the Thirunilam sub-magistrate. It looks like this will blow up into a big incident.'

'Yes, see how he has beaten up this ayya.'

'There's something in that tamarind tree, sir,' offered the constable helpfully.

'There's no damn thing in the tree! You should come around here once a night to patrol the place. Do you have a lamp on your bicycle?'

'Velli, go and bring hot water in a bottle. Ayya can wipe himself down …'

'I'll bring two other stout fellows with me tonight,' offered Marudamuthu. 'If that thief comes again, we will nab him. Ettayya Pillai is a family man. If one falls and something happens to the other, what will the two wives do?'

Ayyadurai laughed uproariously, and totally inappropriately. The constable ticked off Marudamuthu. 'Marudamuthu, just shut up.'

'What's in the bag? Tamarind fruits?' Thangarasu wanted to know.

Velli just stood and glared at Snehalatha.

All these snatches of conversation flowed in a jumble around Kalyanaraman's ears.

As he drank coffee, his throat felt sore. *I'm starting a fever*, he thought. He didn't know when exactly the others left. He went to sleep. By evening, the fever had soared. Snehalatha came over and handed him more pills. Cephalexin, erythromycin … he swallowed pill after pill. A *vaidhyar* visited, felt his pulse and declared, 'It is *pitha naadi*. All due to bile. Starve him. Saar, take this powder mixed in some honey. Some mucus will flow and you will be cured.' He could not eat. Snehalatha's perfume filled his nostrils.

On the second … or maybe it was the third day … the clouds in his mind started clearing a little. His room was a mess. Stale bread, medicine wrappings, the vaidhyar's powder packets, tepid water in a pot. 'Snehalatha!' No answer. But his fever was gone.

His watch had stopped. It was probably afternoon. He was hungry. He got up and started pacing up and down the room. At one end was an ancient wooden cupboard with a rusted lock and fastenings, obviously dating back to the zamindar's days. With time to kill, he walked back and forth between the bed and the cupboard. He drummed his fingers on the door of the cupboard. He tried to pull it away from the wall against which it stood. As it moved, he saw that there was a small door behind it, leading into another room. Excited with the discovery, he pulled the cupboard further away. He pushed the door. It would not budge. It seemed to be fastened on the other side. He leaned his shoulder on it and pushed harder. Encouraged by a kind of crumbling sound from behind the door, he gave it an almighty blow. The lock splintered and the door flew open crookedly. Something was preventing it from opening all the way, but Kalyanaraman manoeuvred his limbs to insert himself through the narrow opening. He looked into the room.

As his eyes adjusted to the dim light, he could make out a jumble of things standing around. An iron cot, a cradle, a child's walker toy with ornate handles; an eclectic collection of pictures … landscapes, Ramar Pattabhishekam, Vini White Rose soap advertisement featuring a White woman … The whole room was cluttered with things, leaving no room for anyone to move about. On the bed lay a jumble of books and piles of notebooks. When he touched them, a small cloud of dust puffed up. 'ACHOO!' he sneezed. He spotted a small photograph; a boy, about ten years old, was standing next to a younger boy, presumably his brother. Both were wearing loose Western-style clothes and staring dutifully into the camera. *One of these was probably Snehalatha's father*, thought Kalyanaraman. Another small photo, this time of Ratnavathy. She wore the same terrified expression as the one in the bigger photo that had hung in the upstairs hall.

He studied the titles of the books. *The Secret of Rathnapuri*, *Digambar Samiyar*, *English–Tamil Vocabulary*, *The Story of Madanakamarajan*, *The Story of Padmavathy*. The historical epic *Soolamani Vasanam* … he opened the book.

'Drumbeats resonated to announce the wedding of Thivitta Nambi and Suyamprabai. Music, dancing and mime marked the lead-up to the auspicious event …'

He closed the book and picked up a notebook. 'On this … day of … I the undersigned have hereby received exactly … rupees and … annas.' He abandoned that notebook and selected another.

'Ratnavathy, Ratna, Rattham.' 'Rattham … blood!' On the page was the mark of a finger dipped in blood. He turned the page. A single line: 'How many days more, Muthamma?' He flipped the page. Again a single line on an otherwise blank page: 'If one were to powder a diamond and swallow it, death will be instant.'

A few pages further along in the book, the pages were densely covered with writing. 'If someone comes across this book many years after I'm gone, I, Ratna, want to tell them my small story.' Was this the actual handwriting of Ratnavathy herself? He plunged into her story eagerly.

> I was born and grew up in a town that lies to the west. Megalapuram. As a child, I was taken in a car to school. Till I was nine my patti fed me from a golden bowl. After I finished Class Four, they decided that was enough. I stopped going to school. I was married before I attained puberty. A very grand wedding. Then I came here. Three pregnancies before I was eighteen. Each time the agony … girl, girl, girl … He drank liquor openly in front of me. There were White women, there was the card-playing … RATNA GOOD GIRL. RATNA NOT HAPPY. He was from a high station in life. I saw him descend to the gutter. All the jewellery my parents had given me …

'Ayya! Ayya!' The sudden loud voice from the front of the house startled him. Kalyanaraman hurriedly hid the notebook, went back into his room and out to the front.

'What is it, Velli? What are you doing here?'

'Did he come here?'

'No, I haven't seen Marudamuthu since this morning.'

'And that woman?'

'No.'

Velli hesitated and bit her lip. She cast her glance downwards.

'What's the matter, Velli?'

'Are you feeling all right now?' she asked.

'Not bad, Velli. Tell me what's going on. You seem to be crying.'

'He has forgotten me, ayya!'

'What do you mean?'

'He comes and goes, but doesn't stop even to exchange a couple of words with me. Every time he says something it is about her. What sort of relationship is it? Just because she is the zamindar's granddaughter, does it mean he has to follow her like a shadow everywhere? Here I am ... a luscious shoot of barnyard millet ... and yet he prefers to go around with that Kurathi.

'Pretending to learn English! They just take some books and disappear into the grove on that accursed cycle. The way that man has lost his senses and fallen under her spell! Her constant laughter and his silly giggling in response before running to buy her some sweet *paniyaram* to please her. I just can't tolerate this any longer. What does he see in the wretched woman that makes him hover around her like this? She has given him some magic powder to make him forget me. She is an evil witch! Pah!' Velli snapped all ten fingers and threw the resulting evil curses towards Snehalatha's door.

'Velli, she is not that kind of woman.'

'What are you saying, ayya! Haven't you seen the kind of shirts she wears? She puts her body on show. Have you ever seen her in a sari? Pah! Such a bow-legged creature! Those rat-like eyes of hers are always searching for male prey. Please try to put some sense into his head. The whole village is talking and laughing about it. Please tell him what he is doing isn't right.'

'Why don't you tell him that yourself, Velli?'

She flinched. 'But he never comes. He has been with her all the time for the past three days. When she comes here I'm going to confront her. I'll say, "Look here, woman! Even if you build a house just across the street and put two windows in it to look at us, my husband is my husband."'

'Your husband?'

'It's been decided at the Panchayat that he will be my husband. So yes, I think of him as my husband. He is the one who is ignoring our relationship. All due to the plotting of that evil woman … that ball of manure! I'm going to confront her.'

With determination writ large on her face, Velli sat on the floor of the verandah. Her whole body was trembling. Tears were ready in her eyes. She bit the beads of her necklace restlessly. She was a wounded tiger, licking her wounds, awaiting the moment to spring at her tormentor.

'Look, Velli, that amma is not an evil woman. She just doesn't know the ways of the village. Women from Madras always talk and laugh and move easily with everyone. You mustn't take it the wrong way.'

'Hah! She is constantly touching him, patting him. They go to the cinema together. He gets back late at night and he is reeking of perfume. I'll wait, di. Where can you go? You have to come home sometime. I'll be waiting for you.'

Kalyanaraman ventured to bring up his own indiscretion. 'Well, if you're talking about that, I too behaved stupidly with you the other day …'

'And what did I do? Did I not stop you dead with one stern word? Why? Because of my feelings for this man, my responsibility for the relationship I have with him, that's why.' She went on to address the absent Marudamuthu.

'Should you not have that same sense of responsibility towards me? So what if she is throwing herself at you? Where is your good sense? You're running after her, grinning, as if you were Kathavarayan. Let her come. I will put an end to this …'

By this time, Velli was muttering the words more to herself. 'My father has found so many possible grooms for me. So many men want to marry me. Men with rings on all ten fingers, wearing big moustaches, driving their own bullock carts. Pah! As if I can't toss away this man in a moment!'

'Why don't you do that?' Kalyanaraman wanted to know.

'My heart won't let me do it. I've known him for such a long time …'

Kalyanaraman was very apprehensive. The moment the two of them arrived, Velli was going to start spewing fire. This young woman's emotional responses were set in old times, more like the Sangam Age. The intense jealousy of a thwarted lover, the fury of a small child who has had her favourite doll taken away from her. Tears flowed. She sniffled. A cycle bell announced the arrival of the missing pair in the drama.

Kalyanaraman froze in tension. Fortunately, Snehalatha was seated behind Marudamuthu, on the carrier. 'Oy! Oy!' she called out, as though to a horse. Marudamuthu applied the brakes and brought the cycle to a halt in front of Velli. He was wearing a shirt with a collar. He was wearing trousers instead of a veshti, and he had combed his curly hair.

'Hi, Velli … sweet girl!' Snehalatha called out.

Velli tucked her sari pallu tightly at her waist and said sternly, 'Get off the cycle, ayya!'

'What's the matter, Velli?' he asked, laughing lightly.

'She is very upset,' announced Kalyanaraman in English for the benefit of Snehalatha.

Velli launched into her speech. 'Amma, you belong to a noble family. You are dragging this man with you everywhere, every day, wherever you go. Does this seem right to you?'

As if someone had thrown a switch, the whole atmosphere of the scene changed in a split second.

'Velli, look here! Think of whom you are talking to, pilla!' Marudamuthu was trying to intercede.

'Shut up!'

'You say *I* am dragging *him* around?'

'Yes, this man is to be my husband.'

'Good, marry him. Congratulations!'

'Velli!' Marudamuthu cautioned her.

'It's not right on your part to go around with him like this.'

'I am going around with him, am I? According to which code of conduct?'

'Touching him, giggling, disappearing into the grove together … in what code of conduct is that all right?'

'Ey, Velli! You mad woman! Moodevi! I'll thrash you …' Marudamuthu raised his hand to land a blow on her.

'Will you dare to raise your hand to me? Will you dare to beat me? I will chop up your arm into tiny bits!'

'Marudamuthu … what are you doing … stop!' urged Kalyanaraman in alarm.

'Ayya, you stay out of this. Don't interfere. Velli, ey, you stupid dumb creature, do you realize who amma is?'

'Wait, Marudamuthu,' said Snehalatha calmly. 'Velli, don't get all worked up with me. It is your man who is keen on being with me all the time. I've never asked him to come and take me anywhere. Understand? If you are feeling upset, get him to behave. Don't shout at me. Do you know my status, you country animal? You're not even equal to the dust on my shoes.'

Velli lashed out through her tears with all the swear words and insults at her command. 'I don't care who you are, di! You slut, loose woman, lump of manure, sewer pipe …'

'Marudamuthu, do I have to listen to this?'

'Yes, you shameless male butterfly!' shouted Velli.

'What did you say, you bloody bitch?' Snehalatha picked up a pebble from the ground and flung it at Velli. It hit her on the forehead.

Marudamuthu rushed and grabbed Velli. He dragged her off the verandah. 'Go home this instant or I will knock out all your teeth!' he threatened, pushing her violently.

Velli fell. Holding a hand over her injured forehead, she told him, 'You are accursed. Can you escape this sin? Will Goddess Mari not punish you? Will Goddess Visalakshi not curse you? Will you not be pierced all over with thick, sharp gunny-bag needles? And won't you bleed through a hundred wounds? Won't your house catch fire …?'

She rose to her feet. '*Inda*, ayya. You dared to hit me! I will ask my father to drag you into the middle of the street and thrash you with a tamarind twig whip.'

'Oh, get lost, di. Your father is a worthless good-for-nothing.'

Velli staggered away, weeping loudly. By then a small crowd of about ten people had collected. 'What happened? What's the matter?'

'Go, get lost! Mind your own business,' scolded Marudamuthu, chasing them away.

Marudamuthu tried to salvage the situation. He stood and smiled sheepishly at Snehalatha.

'Don't smile! I've never been so insulted in my whole life. Go home and don't ever come back.'

'Snehamma, Snehamma, please! She is an ignorant girl. You are educated and wise. Please forgive and forget. I'm ready to fall at your feet and beg you.'

'Ask her to come and fall at my feet. Then we will talk.'

Kalyanaraman was a silent spectator in the whole drama.

10

MARUDAMUTHU HOVERED UNEASILY, UNSURE about what to do next. In a voice trembling with anger Snehalatha said, 'Look at the way that girl talked to me, Kalyanaraman! You probably coached her to talk like that to me.'

'Hey, hold on! Are you now making me the target to continue your quarrel?' protested Kalyanaraman.

Marudamuthu was still desperately trying to defuse the situation. 'Amma, she is an ignorant girl who spoke rubbish. Please just ignore it.'

'What? Get lost! It's all your fault.'

'So I must just get her to come and fall at your feet and ask for your pardon. That's it, right?'

'What do I care! Let her go to hell. I had a good mind to give her a thrashing with my slipper. Absolutely no decency …'

'Amma, I am so miserable about all this. My mind is reeling. I could never have imagined that she would descend to this kind of behaviour. I would have landed a blow on her ear, but because she is a woman I held back …'

'Che, *poyya*! Don't come here again. I came to this village looking for a change for just a week. Just because I talked to a man sociably, I have been made into some kind of villain. I am being labelled a whore and worse. Che, che!'

'Amma, if it is your wish I will cut off all communication with Velli. Just tell me.'

'Why should you cut off your relationship with her? Go ahead and marry her and have eight children. What do I care! Just don't come here again.'

'Amma, please … please don't say that! I can't bear to stay away without seeing you. You are such a noble woman, such a great family … can Velli even hope to be a speck of dust under your feet …' Marudamuthu was overcome with emotion; tears filled his eyes. He sat down right there on the ground. 'Snehamma, I won't stir from here until you assure me that you're not angry with me.'

Kalyanaraman sensed that Snehalatha was secretly enjoying the way this drama was unfolding. Maybe she saw it as a way to take revenge on Velli.

'All right, I am not angry with you. You can leave now.'

'Can I come for English lessons?'

'Mm.'

'You wanted to learn how to drive a tractor …'

'Yes, you can teach me.'

'Can I come and sleep here at nights?'

'Yes, come.'

Marudamuthu swung onto his cycle joyfully and pedalled away.

'Crazy fellow!' remarked Snehalatha.

'No, not crazy. He loves you.'

'And I love you! What's that notebook in your hand? More folk songs?'

'No, something fascinating! It's about your family. It's Ratnavathy's diary. Absolutely riveting …!'

Snehalatha practically leapt at him in her eagerness to snatch the book from his hands. He held the book behind his back. 'Give it! Give it to me!' She clawed at his arms aggressively and snatched the book. Her fingernails left a streak of blood on his arm.

'Ratnavathy is alive in this book. An old woman, Periatha, told me that Ratnavathy committed suicide by hanging. The backdrop to that sad tale is in this diary. I haven't finished reading it yet.'

Snehalatha was not paying any attention to Kalyanaraman. She was totally immersed in the book. Turning the pages slowly, she walked towards her room.

'Will you give me the book when you have finished reading it?'

She stood and thought for a moment. 'It's about family matters. Still, I will let you have it. But only on one condition.'

'I can guess what that condition will be. I refuse.'

'Are you really so cold and insensitive? No, no, you have feelings for a special person. You probably think because she is a village girl she will be "fresh" for your taking. I tell you, that Marudamuthu would have sucked all that freshness out of her by now and she will be used goods.'

'You indulge in absolute gutter talk sometimes!'

'You belong to a high caste and you are lusting after this low-caste girl.'

'You are overstepping your boundary here,' he warned.

She laughed and said, 'In this village I have many admirers. The way they look at me ...! Marudamuthu of course is always hanging around waiting for at least a side glance from me. That Panchayat man Thangarasu ... he went on pestering me to come and see a foreign breed of cow at his place. I did. In the cattle shed he touched my hand and grinned fawningly at me. I told him, "Thangarasu, you're married, right? And you have a daughter around my age? I will tell your wife about how you behaved with me during the visit to the cattle shed. Where is your wife?" "She has gone to the town," he said. "All right," I said, "I will tell her about it after she returns." He looked terrified, like he'd seen a ghost. It turns out he has taken big loans from his father-in-law and is deep in debt. My threat spelt disaster. I tell you, the men in this village are like putty in my hands. Only one is still resisting ...'

'Make me the exception. Leave me alone.'

'How can I let you get away so easily?' she said breezily as she went into her room.

Kalyanaraman thought, *Snehalatha is certainly an attractive woman. Considering the abuse Velli heaped on her, her response seems to be somewhat measured. A person given to easy, carefree laughter, and with an unmistakable Madras polish. Everything seems to be an adventure to her … learning how to drive a tractor, seducing Maduramuthu … these are challenges to be tried and achieved at least once …*

He went into his room. He realized he was hungry, but he found only a couple of slices of dry bread. He had no inclination to start cooking.

'Kalyanaraman, could you please come here a moment?'

He crossed over to her room rather hesitantly. *What is she going to try now?* he wondered.

He found her sitting with the Ratnavathy diary open on her lap. She lifted it up carefully with both hands and held it out to him, open at a particular page.

'Look at this.'

On the page lay a pressed flower, its long, crushed petals staining the pages blood-red.

'Can you identify this flower?'

Kalyanaraman looked at it closely. 'It's a champaka flower,' he told her. He could make out the words in Ratnavathy's handwriting next to the dead flower: 'I have marked the place …' Before he could read further, Snehalatha shut the book with a snap.

'Are you sure it is a champaka flower?'

'Well, they are usually yellow, but this one has been crushed for many, many years and has blackened. Yes, it looks like a champaka.'

'Champaka …' she said meditatively, looking out of the window.

'Why, what is it?'

'Oh, nothing.'

'Did you read it all?'

'No, but I read some of it. Ratnavathy has suffered a lot. That man seems to have been a kind of sadist.'

'But consider the background. He was in awe of all things British. A feudalistic mindset. Then he marries an ignorant, innocent young girl and brings her here. He tries to thrust a totally unfamiliar culture and lifestyle on her. He not only ignores her feelings and desires but openly goes around with a string of women, dancing, carousing ... Have you finished reading it?'

'No, not yet.'

'What about the page with the flower, the one you showed me?'

'I haven't come to that part yet.'

'What does she say about the flower?'

'She writes that she has put her favourite flower in the book to mark an important part of her life. How poetic!'

'Will you let me have the book when you have finished with it?'

A slight hesitation. Then, 'All right.'

'And before that will you give me some biscuits? I'm starving.'

'I will.'

He watched as she placed the book carefully inside her suitcase and locked it.

The next day Kalyanaraman got caught up in a strange village meeting. He was walking along the road towards the thicket of trees when Thangarasu, accompanied by a few other men, approached him.

'Will you please come with us to the peepul tree,' requested Thangarasu.

'Why, what's it about?'

'We heard that fellow Marudamuthu beat up Velli black and blue. You were there, right?'

'Well, he didn't actually beat her, Thangarasu. He told her to go home …'

'But he pushed her, didn't he?'

'Why do you ask?'

'Velli's father has complained to the Panchayat and they are going to enquire about it now. Please come.'

'*Ada* … *da* … why me?'

'Just come and watch. You don't have to say anything.'

'I don't want to be called as a witness or anything like that.'

'Don't worry, just come.'

People were straggling in slowly to the meeting. One of the men was heard saying, 'It is a private matter. The donkey had to be taught a lesson after all …'

When the small knot of people spotted Thangarasu, they fell silent. Most of the men present were bare-bodied.

'Where's Marudamuthu?'

'Someone has gone to fetch him.'

'Marudamuthu must have gone to buy anklets for the zamindar's granddaughter.'

'Shh! *Le*, keep quiet, she may hear you.'

'I hear *Nadodi Mannan* is running in the theatre tent. And they say a man is standing next to the screen and tossing out flowers.'

'Look, the old man is coming. It's best for him to call off this alliance and look for another bridegroom for his daughter.'

'No man in the village will come forward to marry her after this.'

The man who was now approaching the tree must be Velli's father, thought Kalyanaraman. His nose resembled Velli's. He was well-built, blue-veined and muscled. In his banian pocket, near his midriff, a wallet was visible. His hard-soled slippers beat a tattoo on the street as he strode up and seated himself. The gathering fell silent.

'Shall we begin?' asked the sarpanch. 'This year, everyone must contribute five rupees for the *kodai* festival at the temple.'

There was a murmur among the crowd. 'Who is going to do the ritual this year?' asked one of them.

'Marudamuthu.'

'We have to cancel that immediately.'

'But how can we do that? It's already been decided.'

'For what he has done, he does not deserve that privilege. We must remove him.'

'That is different and this matter today is different ...'

'Anna, let Marudamuthu come ...'

'Someone has gone to fetch him. Meanwhile we will attend to the matter of our Kali and his wife. Ayyadurai, please come forward and speak your words of wisdom to them.'

Kali and his wife stood in front of the gathering. Ayyadurai addressed them.

'Between husband and wife there may be many problems and misunderstandings. But it is not good to attack each other physically.'

'She hit me first. She slammed a pot against my forehead,' claimed Kali.

His wife made her case. 'Ayya! This man comes home drunk and indulges in all kinds of atrocities. I can't even begin to describe them. *Enya*, didn't you steal the money I had saved up in the pot? And didn't you thrash our son?'

'Wait, hold on! We have to settle this peacefully. Look, pilla, it's wrong to beat your lawfully wedded husband.' Turning to Kali he said, 'Here, take this *vibhuti* and smear it on your forehead.'

'Give some vibhuti to his wife also,' suggested a voice from the audience.

Marudamuthu arrived along with two companions. He walked towards them, hands folded across his chest.

'*Ennaya*? Why have you called a village meeting?'

'You beat Velli, didn't you?'

'What? I beat her? Which bastard is saying that?'

'Look at the language he is using!'

'You don't know how crudely that girl cursed and abused the zamindar's granddaughter. That ayya standing there was a witness to the whole thing. Ask him.'

All the heads swivelled and all the eyes settled on Kalyanaraman.

As everyone's attention turned on him, Kalyanaraman flinched. Marudamuthu, Velli's father, perhaps Velli herself from some nearby window, and all these villagers were waiting for him to speak. What should he say? 'Just state the facts,' he told himself. 'Just tell them exactly what happened.'

'It's true that Velli came and waited at the zamindar's house and abused the zamindar's granddaughter when she and Marudamuthu arrived. It's also true that Marudamuthu became angry and pushed her so that she fell down.'

'See? The fellow laid hands on my daughter and beat her,' declared Velli's father.

'Hey, I did *not* beat her, ayya,' asserted Marudamuthu.

'When two women are quarrelling, what right do you have to interfere and push one of them to roll on the dust of the floor?'

'Marudamuthu! Why did you touch her? Why did you beat her?' asked someone from the audience.

'Oh shut up, da! Idiot!'

'What sort of language is this! How can you use such words in a village meeting?'

'*Po* da, you gutter rat … etcetera, etcetera.' The target of the abuse sprang angrily at Marudamuthu. The latter just flung him aside casually. Chaos reigned.

Thangarasu drew Marudamuthu aside. The crowd fell silent and listened.

'Marudamuthu, the way you behaved with Velli was wrong. You have to apologize. Plus, for behaving in such a manner, you must pay a fine of one rupee to the Panchayat. What do you all say ...?'

The Panchayat approved the decision. But some voices from the crowd would not be stilled.

'He cannot be allowed to do the kodai ritual at the temple festival this year!'

'True, he must not, he must not!'

'What? I should not be allowed to do the kodai? Look here, Thangarasu, if I reveal right here and now how you behaved with Snehamma, your name will be mud. Anyway, I will not pay any fine. No, no, no fine! And if anyone tries to stop me when I do the kodai, I shall break the fellow's arms and legs.'

Marudamuthu flapped his top cloth vigorously to emphasize his threats, tucked it under his arm and strode away imperiously.

'He is very rebellious. He needs to be disciplined.'

'I will do the kodai ritual,' declared Velli's father. 'Let me see what he will do.'

The crowd had broken up into separate knots of people talking animatedly about the recent goings-on. Kalyanaraman walked away slowly with a troubled mind. People were turning against one another. The arrival of Snehalatha had caused a kind of blight to fall over the village.

He reached the temple and walked past the Pillayar shrine and the sleeping Bioscope Man. As he entered the temple a dreadful sound assailed his ears. And then he came across a sight that made him freeze in horror. A chicken with its head cut off, its reflexes still working through the throes of impending death, was skittering around, small fountains spouting from its open neck, its lifeblood making random kolams on the ground.

11

THE EXPERIENCE OF WITNESSING the headless chicken's dance of death upset Kalyanaraman profoundly. He was made harshly aware that beneath the veneer of modernity in the village lay centuries of outmoded cruel practices, traditions, beliefs, fears …

When the headless bird finally realized it was dead and collapsed in its own blood, the pujari picked it up casually and went into the temple.

'Why?' asked Kalyanaraman. 'Why did you sacrifice that bird?'

'Velli brought it. She asked me to offer it as a sacrifice at the temple so that her troubles may be resolved.'

'Poor thing! What suffering!'

'I know. That girl has suffered a lot.'

'I was talking about the chicken.'

'By now it would have attained the Lord's feet.'

Velli came hurrying in. 'Is it done?' she asked.

'Yes, it's done, Velli.' He smeared chicken blood on her forehead as a blessing. 'You should also visit the temple of the spirits. If any evil spirit is let loose it may make stones rain down. But there's no hurry about that. First I will tell you some other things you should do …'

'Oh, ayya is here!' exclaimed Velli, spotting Kalyanaraman. 'You were at the village meeting. You would have seen how the man talked, how he behaved. Refusing to pay a one-rupee fine to the village! He came and shouted outside the window at our home. Did you hear what he said about the temple kodai ritual? If anyone other than him dares to do it, there will be murder! He threatens to murder my own father! Such words he used to curse me! "Ey, Velli, which fellow will agree to take you as his wife? You sick, sick creature! You dark-skinned creature!" As if he is a white *dorai*! He comes and shouts at me like this. I'm miserable. He never used to talk this way. That wretched concubine and her crotch …! She is the one who has made him behave like this. Do you think I'll let her get away with it? I will finish her off once and for all. Wait and see! That *eeruvali kuchi* woman … yes, that's what she's like … a stick for combing out hair lice! She's turned up here like a newly hatched cobra …'

During this outburst from Velli, Periatha had joined them. She said, 'Ennadi, I hear she is saying all kinds of things. She says your man will marry her.'

'Hah! You think I will let her do that?'

'Four makilam flowers, forty-eight roses!' Periatha had words of caution for Velli. 'The flower that you were holding close to you and fondling is now being fondled by someone else. That's what has hit you, Velli. You were the very essence of the aromatic vetiver sold at the Chettys's shop; you were the fragrant rose water of Sivakasi. How did you get transformed into this avatar of Moodevi?'

'It's my fate, Periatha. So many offers of marriage came for me, from Megalapuram, Pandiapuram … But Marudamuthu lives right here, a known man with a steady farming job, so my father said yes. He consented to the alliance. But now he has forbidden him from entering the house!'

'Tell me honestly, Velli,' said Kalyanaraman, 'how do you feel about Marudamuthu? Do you hate him now?'

Velli seemed stunned by the question. Her eyes roved restlessly from side to side as she gathered her thoughts. 'Me? I don't … know,' she said hesitantly. 'I don't know what I feel.'

'Let that witch's evil plans be defeated. Then things will become clear,' declared Periatha. 'Ayya, I came here now only to meet you.'

'Oh, all right. Let's go to the house …' said Kalyanaraman, moving away. Periatha fell in step beside him, and the two of them walked towards the house. Kalyanaraman went into his room and Periatha followed, talking all the while.

'That woman is a no-good creature, ayya. She may be the zamin's family but she is wicked. Poor Velli, how she has been suffering …'

'You have lost half your hearing and now even half your senses, it seems. Just come quietly.'

'If you can give me a rupee I can buy a measure of rice and …'

Kalyanaraman sighed. 'All right.'

In the open area at the left of the zamindar's mansion, the tractor was bouncing up and down and running in random circles like a young child at play. At the wheel was Snehalatha, and standing next to her, balanced precariously, was Marudamuthu, applying the steering corrections that were often required because of her excessive exuberance. Snehalatha's merry laughter had drawn Kalyanaraman's attention to this new drama. As he stepped outside to watch, she spotted him and drove the tractor full tilt towards him. As he hurriedly stepped aside, she laughed some more, and brought the vehicle to a halt.

'Do you want to try your hand at driving this?'

'No.'

By now Periatha had come into view. Snehalatha greeted her, 'Hi, old woman!' Then, to Kalyanaraman, 'Who's this? New girlfriend?'

Snehalatha was seated on the tractor seat as though she were royalty on a throne. Marudamuthu jumped to the ground. 'Amma has learnt to drive in no time at all,' he remarked.

'I heard there was a Panchayat meeting about me?' asked Snehalatha.

'It wasn't about you,' responded Kalyanaraman.

Marudamuthu cut in. 'Ayya, did you hear the sort of things Velli's father said? She must have gone and told him some exaggerated story about what happened and he rushed to call a village meeting! He could have confronted me directly, right? Why a public meeting? Only to humiliate me, isn't it? And they want me to pay a fine! Am I a wicked man, Periatha?'

At this point, Periatha executed a volte-face that stunned Kalyanaraman. She joined forces with the opposite camp!

'Useless fellows with nothing else to do! That's why they call these village meetings. After all, she is the granddaughter of the zamindar. What's wrong if you show her around the place? Look at her! Like a rose. My darling, my little calf . . .!'

Kalyanaraman stepped into the conversation. 'Still, Marudamuthu, you should behave the way people expect of you. Maybe your intentions are pure, and so are this amma's intentions. But Velli is a simple, illiterate girl whom you are to marry. Look at it from her point of view.'

'Marry her? Who's going to marry her now?'

'What do you mean?'

'Neither will I marry her nor will I allow anyone else to marry her. I will tear any such fellow limb from limb.'

'Shabash! Hurrah!' exclaimed Snehalatha.

'What? Shabash? You don't know what you're talking!' protested Kalyanaraman.

'Let her grow old as a spinster.'

'Don't be ridiculous!'

'Tell me, why are you so anxious to get Marudamuthu hitched up with Velli? Surely you should be happy if they break up?'

He stopped her with a stern glance. 'Why are you exploiting Marudamuthu?' he demanded in English, hoping to keep that part of the conversation only between them. But she responded in Tamil. 'He is the one who is seeking me out. Also, is it a sin to learn to drive a tractor?'

'Village folks become aggressive even about small matters. They resort to physical violence.'

'Is that so? But then I have a bodyguard! So why should I be afraid? What do you say, Marudamuthu?'

'I won't allow anyone to lay a finger on you, amma. We are a team. Even if the whole village is against us, I will manage. I'll just get behind the wheel of the tractor and drive it at full speed, straight … What do you say, Periatha?'

'She looks lovely, like a ripe fruit. And royal blood in her too. So what if someone goes with her to show her a couple of places and helps her drive a tractor? Those idle fellows and their wagging tongues! Donkeys, the whole lot of them! They will talk, so let them talk.'

'Marudamuthu,' said Snehalatha, 'don't forget what we have agreed on.'

'Sure, amma, it will be done.'

'What have you agreed on?' asked Kalyanaraman.

'Er … that is …' Marudamuthu hesitated in confusion.

'Shh! Don't breathe a word about it to this ayya,' warned Snehalatha.

'Oh? I couldn't care less!' declared Kalyanaraman.

But of course Snehalatha had to have her moment. 'Marudamuthu and I are going together to a secret place. Isn't that so, Marudamuthu?'

'Yes, amma.'

'We are going to pluck flowers. Champaka flowers!' They exchanged meaningful glances and started laughing.

'*Rasa … thi!* She laughs exactly the way Ratnamma used to laugh!' cackled Periatha.

With Periatha the turncoat traitor trailing in his wake, Kalyanaraman went back into his room. The moment she reached the doorway, Periatha sat down and started crooning:

'Near Thiruchendur, on the Virichathalai bridge,
Those vows that were exchanged in all good faith
Lie crumbled to dust.'

'Periatha, please, no songs today. Here's a rupee. Buy your measure of rice and your malli coffee and get a new waist string for the baby.'

'Bless you! You are a prince. In this messy situation, your stand is the right one. Marudamuthu must behave the way society expects him to. Even if the two of them have no bad intentions, all this touching and patting ... how can they openly do that?'

'Periatha, you should have been in *arasiyal* ... politics! You can argue both ways!'

'Arasai ilai ... peepul leaves? All right, I'll pluck some for myself. And some drumstick leaves too.'

With the sounds of the tractor and Snehalatha's loud laughter still echoing outside, Kalyanaraman decided to take a quick peep into her room through the window. He saw Ratnavathy's diary on a stool fairly close to the window. He found it within reach, so he stealthily grabbed it and hurried back to his room with it. He sat on his bed, opened the book to the page where he had left off reading earlier when he had been interrupted, and picked up the thread of Ratna's story.

> There is no one who will weep for me. My children are too young to understand anything. This house is very large, but ... that's all that is left. He squandered all his inherited wealth on pleasing the White people and buying gifts for

them. His vanity drove him to seek some kind of position in government; he thought he could buy status that way. He stood for election to the Panchayat Board. He even hired a plane to drop advertising leaflets on the streets and gifted a silk sari and a gold coin to every household. He lost the election. He had frittered away all his assets, everything turned to dust. Peace! But then the moneylenders have started to come, and the storekeepers who had sold him things on credit. So now he is asking me to part with my jewellery.

These jewels were handed down for generations, from my great-great-grandmother. Gold melted, fashioned and polished, beautifully designed and carefully studded with precious stones. What right did I have to give them away? 'The moneylender is at the door and I have to answer him,' he said, 'so give me your jewels. I will pledge them, redeem them later and return them to you.' Pah! Like offering a hungry elephant a handful of puffed corn! 'Go and sell this house and your lands,' I told him. 'I won't part with my jewels.' I don't know from where I got the courage to stand up to him like that. I was hurt. He cared about those wretched jewels, but what about me? He didn't seem to care for me at all. Am I just some inanimate frame on which jewels are draped? Is that all I am? Don't I have feelings, desires, a right to dignity, a right to a good life?

He took out his whip. This time I said, 'Go ahead, beat me!' He ripped the clothes off my back. He screamed in rage, raised his whip and brought it down hard on my back. It felt as though I had been scalded. The pain was somewhere in the centre of my consciousness. I didn't actually feel it much on my back where the whip landed. I laughed after the whip bit into my back. 'I will kill you!' he growled and stormed away.

Ever since I entered this house, have you ever looked at me affectionately, addressed me as 'dear one'? What right do you have to demand my jewellery?

At this point in the narrative, two words had been blotted out on the page, apparently by tears. It went on:

> Visalakshi Muthamma! What did I get from praying to you every day? I only got whip scars on my back. 'Bend!' he would order me, and I would bend. But I will not bend any more. I have come to a decision. I will not give my jewels to anyone. No rogue or rascal should get his hands on them. My husband should not have them. I've made a plan. I will collect all my jewels together and ...

The diary was snatched out of his hand. He had been so absorbed in Ratna's story that he had not noticed Snehalatha's arrival. He turned around, thoroughly startled.

'So you decided to steal my grandmother's diary from my room when I was away? You also need to be judged at a Panchayat meeting,' she said accusingly.

'But I was the one who found it first,' protested Kalyanaraman.

'That doesn't give you the right to read it, does it? How far did you get?'

'I have come to the part where the zamindar is forcing her to part with her jewellery.'

'Oh, only that far? That's a relief!'

'Why do you say that?'

'I've finished reading all of it.'

'What happens later? How does it end?'

'I'll give it to you later and you can read for yourself.'

'I know that you will never give it to me.'

'Why?'

'Because you are trying to hide something.'

'What do you mean?'

She tried to sound casual but her trademark wide smile was missing. Kalyanaraman told her, 'From the very first day I've been watching you closely. You pretend to be naïve and carefree, but in every one of your actions I could detect an underlying determination, the fact that you have a hidden agenda. You did not want me to read the diary. That was very obvious. Your behaviour with Marudamuthu, fooling around with him and teasing him, is also part of your plan. Of course I could be wrong …'

Snehalatha was silent for a while; she seemed to be trying to come to a decision about something. Finally, she said, 'Mister Kalyanaraman, shall I tell you why I didn't want you to read the diary?'

'All right, if you want to.'

'Ratnavathy did not commit suicide. She must have been murdered by the zamindar.'

'Really? Why do you say so?'

'It's plain from reading what she has written. Night after night he tried to force her to part with her jewels. He beat her, whipped her. One night things went too far …' After a brief moment to collect her thoughts she went on. 'I didn't want you to know all the details about how evil my ancestor was …'

'I understand.'

'Mister Kalyanaraman, I have no secrets and no agenda. Please understand, I am an open book. Would you like to read?'

As she spoke, she looked up at him, eyes wide and full of hidden meanings.

'If you mean the diary, yes I would.'

'See, now you are back to your stiff self! Come on, Kalyanaraman!'

'I'm sorry, Snehalatha. You are an attractive woman, but under these circumstances I don't feel we should … let's just be friends.'

'A proper madman you are!' she declared and strode away.

Kalyanaraman chuckled inwardly. *There may be something in what she says*, he thought. *Otherwise why am I not grabbing an opportunity that has so easily come my way?*

He still wasn't convinced that she was everything she claimed to be. He sensed something hidden beneath that apparently innocent surface. But what exactly was she hiding?

A bit of dialogue he had heard came back to him. Snehalatha had said, 'Marudamuthu and I are going to a place where we can pluck champaka flowers.' And just yesterday she had pointed to the faded pressed flower in a page of the diary and asked him what flower it was …

A champaka!

Marudamuthu arrived to spend the night as usual on the verandah. 'Snehamma, I've brought what you wanted.'

Kalyanaraman's curiosity was aroused. What had he brought? He looked through the window.

Marudamuthu was showing Snehalatha a length of thick, twisted rope like those used for drawing water from wells.

12

SNEHALATHA WAS TALKING WITH Marudamuthu, both speaking in low voices. Kalyanaraman couldn't think why Marudamuthu had brought a length of stout rope. He watched as the two of them seemed to arrive at a decision. They set off together purposefully. He was more convinced than ever that the events of the past few days hid some dark secret.

Kalyanaraman lay awake for a long time, troubled by thoughts and images which he could not explain. The champaka flower, pressed to death among the pages of the diary, scratched at the edges of his consciousness; blood from the headless chicken's neck bubbled obscenely in front of his mind's eye. Was his vague sense of anxiety related to these mental images? He could not be sure. He drifted off to sleep and didn't know when the missing pair returned.

The next morning Thangarasu came and announced that a decision had been taken about the traditional temple ritual. Velli's father had been designated as the person who would conduct the ritual at this year's festival.

'But Marudamuthu might raise a ruckus!'

'No, no, he has agreed to it. But he still refuses to pay the one-rupee fine, so we have decided to boycott him.'

'Do you mean Marudamuthu actually agreed to this new arrangement about the temple ritual?' Kalyanaraman was astonished.

Snehalatha emerged from her room. 'It was I who told him to agree without making a fuss. I told Marudamuthu that he shouldn't get into a quarrel with the village because of me.'

'One word from amma is enough for Marudamuthu,' remarked Thangarasu. 'He will abide by her wishes in everything. It's good that you spoke to him about it, amma. You have helped to avoid problems in the village.'

'And what about your wife, Thangarasu? Has she returned from the town?'

Thangarasu squirmed uneasily. 'Amma is always joking about something ...'

'No, no, I'd like to meet your wife. Why don't you bring her here one of these days?'

Thangarasu smiled sheepishly and changed the subject. 'Actually I came about something else. The temple festival will go on for ten days. There will be *villu paatu*, *karagam*, *naiyaandi melam* and *oyil kummi*. Shanmugam will be coming from the Junction. Ayya, I heard you've been teaching the small children to sing together. You must come and make them sing on the first day of the festival. The collector dorai will be coming. He will be very happy to see that.'

'Let's see,' said Kalyanaraman.

'Oh, the Kalyanaraman Symphony Orchestra! Great! What about me? I can dance. Monkey, Jerk, Shake ... May I also join in?'

'Of course. You are a must, amma.'

'I can whistle "WHEE" and I can clap loudly too. Ayya, may I always remain in your good graces.' She executed a mock bow prayerfully to Thangarasu and laughed merrily.

'But I heard that you were planning to leave soon, amma.'

'Oh, so you want to know why I'm still here? I'll go, I'll go. In a few days.'

'When does the festival begin?' asked Kalyanaraman.

On Friday, a pandal stood to the left of the Amman temple. On the open ground, a flimsy metal carousel rotated slowly. There were attractions aplenty. A smiling 'serpent girl' with a human head and a snake's body; a two-headed goat, both fascinating and revolting. Little children wore *javvu mittai* (colourful chewy candy) watches. Bioscope Pazhaniandi was busy with house-full shows. A loudspeaker on a pole blared music; the aroma of yesterday's fish curry shouted in its own language. Under a roughly rigged-up shelter of sacking, peanuts mixed in hot sand leapt up and down in huge pans on the fire; on carts fitted with bicycle wheels, bhajjis and fish fingers sizzled in hot oil. There were stalls for plastic rings, saris going for twenty-something rupees; a stall for pump sets. Stalls with fortune tellers who claimed to predict your future from the card you touched; *madana kamarajan* ... the art of love, illustrated in sixty-four semi-tone prints ...

And nonstop music. Songs of social clubs, political parties, movie songs ...

By evening, the villagers had assembled facing the temple. A drumroll announced the beginning of the festival ... *thom-thum-tha-thom-thum-tha*. The priest had oiled his moustache. Amman stood revealed in all her splendour. She was dressed in grand clothes and bedecked in jewellery and flowers and garlands.

Around a makeshift stage open on three sides, decorations waved in the breeze. On the stage stood Anandayi, Abhirami, Muthu, Karuppayi, Pichai and Esakki, the six children who formed Kalyanaraman's 'orchestra'. Pichai on the *jalra*, Esakki as the kerosene-tin 'double space' player, Muthu and Karuppayi as the vocalists, and the others as chorus-singers-cum-coconut-shell-violinists. Behind them stood Kalyanaraman with his guitar. Thangarasu grabbed a mike. *Scree ... ee ... ch*! 'Quiet! Quiet!' his voice boomed out.

Snehalatha chose that moment to make a stylish entrance. The audience went 'ooh' and 'aah'. 'Are you ready?' she asked Kalyanaraman.

'Well I am a little nervous.'

Thangarasu approached. 'Where is Marudamuthu?' Snehalatha wanted to know.

'He refused to come. He is hiding away and watching everything secretly.'

'There will be no disruptions, right?'

'We can't say. Someone might decide to let loose a donkey into the crowd to create a ruckus. We have the police here just in case.'

'Nothing like that will happen,' declared Snehalatha. 'By the way, Thangarasu, is your wife here in the crowd?'

'I have to go now, amma,' said Thangarasu hastily. 'I have many things to do.'

'Look how the fellow took to his heels,' laughed Snehalatha. 'In his cowshed ...'

'I know, I know, he showed you the English cow, etc. You told me that story.'

'How come you never offer to take me and show me an English cow?'

'Silence! Silence! Till the chief guest arrives our own Sokkan will play tapes.'

'*O pot-bellied Vinayaka, O tiger-skin-clad Sankara, come, come ...*'

The collector duly arrived, a newly appointed young IAS officer in a closed-collar coat, hair neatly combed and altogether shiny and bright. He greeted everyone and smiled and chatted with Snehalatha. Then he was led to the seat of honour, a bamboo-woven chair brought from Thangarasu's house. Next to him sat Snehalatha. Off to one side, wearing shirts in honour of the occasion instead of their usual bare-bodied look, sat Ayyadurai and the Panchayat officials.

'Members of the audience! Now our respected visitor from Madras, Kalyanaraman Iyer, will make our children sing.'

Kalyanaraman's hour had arrived. The musicians were lined up on the stage. Suddenly, stray calls broke out from the audience. 'Ey, Samya!' 'Ey, Karuppayi!' 'Muthu!' The children in the audience were excited to see their friends on the stage. Overwhelmed by the sudden attention, the members of the orchestra chewed their shirts and new ribbons nervously. 'Begin!' called Kalyanaraman. In a small voice, Karuppayi sang, '*Chinna chinna ...*' Kalyanaraman played two chords on his guitar. The unfamiliar vibrations hung in the air. The audience fell silent.

> '*Chinna chinna kayai thatti* . . .
> *We go clap clap with our little hands (clap, clap, clap)*
> *We have learnt a little bit* (Esakki on the kerosene tin: *Thom thom thom*!)
> *With our coconut shell violin* (Muthu scraping out the only two notes he had been taught: *njee* . . . *njee*).'

(Laughter from the audience)

> '*With a rattle of our pots and pans* (Samban providing *thagara ... dagara ... thagara ... dagara* right on cue).'

As the children hit their stride and their voices rose in harmony, the audience listened spellbound. Karuppayi finished with a wide, endearing smile. Kalyanaraman glowed with pride. Snehalatha signalled a thumbs-up sign and mouthed, 'Tops!'

As the music died away, the whole village erupted in applause. *Surely Velli must be somewhere in the audience*, thought Kalyanaraman.

Snehalatha came forward and shook Kalyanaraman's hand so heartily that it was actually painful. The collector added his appreciation. 'Remarkable, Mr Kalyanaraman! I decided right away that I will donate a set of new clothes to each of those children.' He looked at his watch. 'I have an engagement at seven. I must leave now. Snehalatha, we must meet again.' And then he was gone.

It was now time for the villu paatu (bow song) to commence. A *ghatam*, a spherical mud pot, was brought onto the stage and placed carefully on a ring-shaped pad of twisted hay for stability. Then came the long-stringed bow-shaped instrument, the *villu*, that gives the folk music genre its name. At one end of it hung a cluster of tiny bronze bells designed to sway and tinkle when the bow-string is plucked. The main artiste swept onto the stage and seated himself behind the villu. Another settled down behind the ghatam. The *udukku* and jalra percussionists joined them. It was a tight squeeze on the small stage.

'*Jalang*,' sang the villu as the artiste tested the pitch. The ghatam artiste tapped a flat plantain stem on the mouth of the pot. It responded with a deep, rumbling timbre. The other percussionists ensured they were in tune. It was time to launch into song.

> '*From the ancient town of Thenpavazham,*
> *Steeped in the three forms of Tamil,*
> *Comes the story of Iyakki, the story of Iyakki.*
> *My tongue tells the story as I know it*
> *I sing! I sing!*'

The villu paatu artiste's voice soared, the bow-string sang, the percussionists added a mesmerizing '*thakkadaga thangadaga … thakkadaga thangadaga*' rhythm. Kalyanaraman felt goosebumps. He found a chair, set up his tape recorder and pressed the 'record' button.

A bystander said, 'He is singing the Pazhayanur Neeli story. The dead of night witnesses destruction … being torn in two. Very interesting story. What's that box?'

'It's a tape recorder.'

The Story of Pazhayanur Neeli

The Pazhayanur Neeli story is famous as a villu paatu staple all over Tirunelveli district of Tamil Nadu. There are several versions of this story, and here I will relate one of them. A Brahmin named Velavan marries Neeli. Within a few months of marriage, he falls under the spell of a prostitute and leaves his young wife. One day, the prostitute comes to Velavan's home, but Neeli shuts the door in her face. The woman is consumed with fury. When Velavan comes to her the next time, she tells him that she will have nothing more to do with him unless he brings her the *thaali* from his wife's neck.

Velavan goes home and manages to persuade Neeli that he is now a changed man who wants to make amends for his behaviour. He proposes that they go away together and settle in a new town. The trusting Neeli is won over, and agrees to go away with him. On their way through an uninhabited wooded area, they stop near a well. Velavan makes amorous advances to Neeli, sweet-talking her into a state of languor. He picks up a heavy stone and smashes her head, killing her instantly. He tears the thaali away from her lifeless body. But Velavan does not live long to savour the success of his plan, because a serpent slithers up and bites him. Velavan dies.

Here the story jumps seamlessly into the next birth of the two main characters. Neeli, the cheated wife, is craving revenge. At the doors of Kailasa she petitions Lord Siva to allow her to avenge her death at the hands of her murdering husband, and he graciously agrees. Hence she is reborn as the daughter of the Chola king. Velavan, meanwhile, undergoing a change of caste, is reborn as the son of a Chettiar in Kaveri Poompattinam.

Even as a child, Neeli was in the habit of climbing out of her crib, going to the cowshed, and killing and eating cows. In agony and desperation, her father, the king, takes her deep into a forest and leaves her. Neeli grows up in the forest, waiting, waiting …

Meanwhile, Velavan gets married. After his father dies, he wishes to accumulate more wealth. In pursuit of riches he makes his way into a forest. It is the forest where Neeli has been waiting. She assumes the form of a beautiful, captivating maiden and confronts Velavan. 'I am your wife,' she tells him. 'We have a son together.'

'No, no,' protests Velavan, utterly terrified by this turn of events, 'your husband is some other man, not me.' The argument rages on; the two of them decide to consult the opinion of elders. They arrive at Pazhaya Nallur and place the issue before the elders. The latter, after much wise thought and debate, declare that Velavan is indeed Neeli's husband and should therefore live with her.

They are allotted a house in which to spend the night. Neeli cracks open Velavan's chest and drinks his blood. Yet even this is not enough to satisfy the pent-up rage of a woman scorned. She is satiated only after she has killed another seventy people. Once done with the revenge, she becomes an Amman, a goddess, the rewarder of good deeds and the punisher of evil.

Kalyanaraman had been so totally immersed in the absorbing narrative of the villu paatu that he had been unaware of the happenings around him. When he looked around, he saw that Snehalatha was missing from her seat. The ambient light was sufficient for him to see her standing a little distance away, talking to Marudamuthu.

The song was gathering pace, with each line punctuated by a chorus of 'AAMA', 'YES'.

'*When she noticed he was carrying money … AAMA*
She picked up a lamp and led him … AAMA
Come, lie down with me, she said … AAMA
And brought him to her bed … AAMA.'

Snehalatha finished talking to Marudamuthu and moved away into the darkness. Marudamuthu glanced around here and there with a guilty air for a couple of moments and then got onto his bicycle and sped away in the same direction.

'*She brought him to her bed … AAMA*
With its soft feather mattress … AAMA
With stealthy cajoling she persuaded him … AAMA
To shed his clothes … AAMA.'

Kalyanaraman spotted Velli for the first time that evening. She was seated on the ground in the midst of a group of women. She must have been watching Marudamuthu and Snehalatha, because she was looking in that direction.

'*Stay with me, she told him,*
Using her wiles to pour poison in his ears.
From that very day he began to fade
In health of body and strength of mind.'

Velli said something to the woman sitting next to her. She wrung her hands and looked again and again into the darkness where the two had disappeared.

'I grew up believing you would be my husband,
And our elders said we would be man and wife;
Now if you abandon me
Which man will take me in marriage?'

Velli bit at her necklace and nervously slipped her bangles off her wrist and then on again, repeatedly.

'Let us get back together, I will be true to you
Let us give our relationship a chance.'

Now Kalyanaraman could see Velli's eyes. They held uncertainty, anxiety, anger …

'I have known renown in my time,
And temples and palaces too;
But now I'm a mere football kicked around in the street,
My matted hair a stringy disgrace.'

Velli rose from where she had been sitting.

'I am the right woman for you, O Chettiar!
If you embrace me you will know it's true;
In this lifetime you will be mine.

No, don't try to bind me with your love chains, sly woman,
Go away, di, go away!'

Velli wove her way through the crowd and came to the edge of the gathering.

'That's where you and I lived together;
Look, look, there it is.'

Velli stood still for several moments. She seemed to hesitate. Then, with a determined air, she strode in the direction in which the other two had left minutes earlier.

'*Thandana thana, thandana thana, thana thana …*'

The villu twanged, the ghatam bellowed, the udukku and jalra joined in boisterously. The percussion reached a crescendo.

'*He quietly picked up a stone and*
Hurled it at the young woman's head.
She twisted and screamed and rolled on the ground
Her crushed head felt as though fried in hot oil
As the life drained from her she muttered
O Nizhal Ninra Kali, you will bear witness to this!
O Lord Sivasankara, you will bear witness to this!
She said, as she was dying …
As she was dying …'

Kalyanaraman's attention was torn between the musical story unfolding on the stage and the real mystery unfolding in the here and now. Where could they be going at this hour? After all, the whole village was here; every house would be locked, all the streets would be deserted. The moon hung low in the sky. The notes of the villu paatu filled the air all around, travelling well beyond the village grounds. First Snehalatha had slipped away. And then Marudamuthu. Next Velli … then only the darkness.

'*The Amman in human form sprang upon his chest*
And split it wide open
The splattered blood ran in a long stream
Of slush in the dust of the street …'

Splattered blood … slush of the street …

Kalyanaraman experienced a flutter of dread.

13

'I HAVE TOLD YOU THIS story as our forefathers have passed it on to us,' announced the villu paatu singer as his tale drew to an end. The instruments fell silent. By the time the final prayers were done it was one o'clock in the morning. The artistes attended to their coughs and sniffles and returned their instruments to their covers. The audience, swathed in blankets, which had sat huddled in front of the stage for hours, yawned widely and rose slowly to its feet. Kalyanaraman put on a sweater, slipped the cassette out of the recorder and prepared to walk back.

A stranger fell into step beside him. 'It is said that when a villu paatu is scheduled, even the temple lamps will stay unlit. These things sometimes go on into the early hours. I've heard plenty of these ... Sudalaimadan, Marudanayagam Palli, Chinnathambi stories, all these and more. I can also sing.'

'Oh, all right.'

'Shall I come and sing for you? You can record me?'

'Come tomorrow.'

'Ayya, if you can spare a rupee or two ...'

'Sorry, I don't have any change on me. Come tomorrow and I will give it to you.'

'For what amount do you want change?'

'Let us talk about that after you come and sing.'

'All right, ayya, I'll come tomorrow,' said the stranger, moving away into the dark shadows. The occasional pinpoints of light from lamps were like stars fallen out of the sky.

Kalyanaraman walked alone, tortured by anxious thoughts. *Where did those three people go? Excitement! Danger! Marudamuthu and Snehalatha may have gone back to the zamindar house. And then …? Velli comes there and sees the two of them? Doing what? What would have happened then?*

Kalyanaraman's slippers scuffed the dead leaves on the street ... *sarak, sarak* ... in the otherwise still night. His own footsteps seemed to sound a warning. The thought of what may be awaiting him gave him goosebumps. *Some impending monstrous event … a disaster …* The zamin house came into view. In the pale light of the moon floating in the black ocean of sky, the silvery outline of the house was like an apparition in a nightmare. Like a single eye, the window of Snehalatha's room glowed in the darkness. It was the only light that had been turned on. Night insects whirred.

What an eerie setting! This is where the unhappy Ratnavathy lived and died; and this too is where her granddaughter Snehalatha has come. What a contrast between the two women! I must finish reading Ratnavathy's story. I must demand firmly, 'Give me the diary since you have finished reading it. I have a right to read it because I was the one who found it.' Let's see if she is still awake.

Sarak … sarak … sarak … he walked towards her window. Suddenly, tree branches shook noisily nearby, and there came the sound of fleeing footsteps that faded into the distance. It would be impossible to chase anyone through the dark. Perhaps it was Marudamuthu?

'Who was that, Snehalatha?' he called out as he approached her window.

Only a faint echo of his own words reached his ears in response.

He looked through her window and was met by a bizarre sight. A small, puppet-like doll stood near the window. It was made of cloth and twisted rope, and had been draped with a sari, a remnant of coloured cloth. Through its heart was driven a large, sharp darning needle. From her portrait propped against the far wall, Ratnavathy stared with terror in her eyes. No one was in the room.

He went around to the doorway to her room. A mound of holy ash lay strewn on the floor. He opened the door of the room … and saw a bloodstain on the floor. He froze in fear. The stain, about the width of a human hand, was still new. The blood had not yet dried. 'Snehalatha!' he called out. And then louder, 'SNEHALATHA!!' Only distant echoes of his own voice. Again the rustle of tree branches somewhere …

Kalyanaraman left Snehalatha's room and stood and thought for a while. His whole body was still trembling with the shock of seeing the voodoo doll and the blood. He looked around and found spots of blood on the front steps. He went into his own room, picked up a flashlight and prepared to follow the bloodstains wherever they may lead. Flashing the narrow beam of light ahead of him, he followed the trail. His heart thudded in his chest, pumping terror through his body. The blood trail led out into the garden, past the tamarind tree, through an overgrown patch of scrub and towards the old well.

Kalyanaraman swung the flashlight in circles around the area. Dense weeds and shrubs; the crumbling wall at the edge of the well; a hand; a pile of stones …

Wait! A hand! He brought the beam sharply back on the hand and moved it fearfully further. The light moved from hand to elbow to chest … to face. Snehalatha's face!

'Oh my God!'

Her open eyes looked skyward and her jaw hung loose, a smear of blood at the corner of her mouth. Her posture was ungainly, half sitting and half lying, with one leg stretched out and the other bent.

Snehalatha! The beam of light jumped about erratically as Kalyanaraman's hand trembled. What should he do? He approached her and touched her gently. 'Snehalatha,' he called gently, 'look here, Snehalatha.' He patted her cheek, trying to wake her. Her head shook loosely, and another thin stream of blood emerged from her mouth and dripped down.

'AYYO!' he screamed, as reality sank in. He turned and ran as fast as he could back towards the village. A stray dog started chasing him, barking aggressively. He picked up a stone and hurled it at the dog. Then his slipper gave way. He ran barefoot, driven by terror, sweating profusely, heart hammering and lungs on overdrive. He came to a stop at the main street of the village and shouted as loudly as his strained lungs would permit: 'Marudamuthu! Thangarasu! Someone, please come at once.' Totally exhausted, he sank to the ground.

Many other dogs seemed to have sensed that first dog's indignation at being targeted with a flung stone. They started barking in chorus.

'Periasamy! Thangarasu! Marudamuthu!' Kalyanaraman picked up a large pebble and threw it against the closed front door of a house. A child started crying. Voices of people roused from sleep: 'Who ...?' 'What . . .?' 'Who . . .?'

'Here, on the main street. Hurry! Hurry!'

'Oh, it's the Madras Ayya! Why are you sitting here on the street, ayya?'

'In the zamindar's house . . . in the garden . . .'

Late in the night the group arrived near Snehalatha's body. They were carrying bamboo canes, hurricane lamps, torches. Kalyanaraman's memory of his earlier encounter with her lifeless body continued to weigh heavily on him. Snehalatha . . . Snehalatha . . . his mental images of her beauty, her childlike way of talking, her gait were superimposed on the ghastly vision of her blood-smeared dead face.

'Snehamma!' Marudamuthu's heart-rending cry echoed all around. He sobbed aloud, shuddering uncontrollably. 'Oh God! What is this! The zamin's granddaughter ...'

Meanwhile, others had been carrying out a close examination of the body.

'Thangarasu! Someone has murdered her, ayya. It is murder! The back of her head has been crushed. Send word to Ayyadurai. Is Periasamy here?'

'Yes, I'm here, ayya.'

'Why are you hiding there at the back? Come here and help lift her.'

'It's a Friday, a holy day, and yet Amman has snatched a life. What made her so angry?'

'This amma was sitting and watching the villu paatu. I saw her there.'

'Yes, she arrived with Marudamuthu.'

Marudamuthu said, between sobs, 'Yes, I took her there. But later she said, "Marudamuthu, you can go now." She asked me to go.'

'Annai, shall we fetch a rope cot ...?'

'No, we can lift and carry her. Hold her now ... listen, I'm telling you to hold this end and lift. What are you afraid of? Periasamy, you come.'

'Stand back, everyone!' Marudamuthu strode forward, scooped up Snehalatha's body in his arms and rested her head on his shoulder. 'Were you looking for some auspicious time to pick her up? Let's get moving.'

'Careful, the path is full of stones.'

Snehalatha's head lolled loosely on Marudamuthu's shoulder and her dead eyes stared sightlessly at nothing.

'Let's take her back to her room.'

'Is she dead?' someone wanted to know.

'No, she's sleeping! You dumb idiot!'

'I said all along that it isn't a good idea to start with that Neeli story. Now we have to do some atonement rituals …'

The footsteps of a dozen men trampled dry leaves underfoot … *sarak, sarak*. Points of light from the lamps and torches danced erratically in the enveloping darkness. Snehalatha's arm hung limply, and with each step that Marudamuthu took, the glass bangles that she had bought that first day in town tinkled on her wrist.

They arrived at the house and went to Snehalatha's room.

'What is this on the floor? Holy ash? Why?'

They went in. Marudamuthu laid Snehalatha gently on the floor. Ratnavathy's terrified eyes in her portrait took in the scene. Was there a subtle hint of something more now in that gaze? 'Che, don't imagine things,' Kalyanaraman chided himself.

Jumbled thoughts ran through his mind as he recollected all the times they had interacted during those few days. *Snehalatha, who wanted you dead? And why? Just hours ago you were full of energy and brimming with life.*

He had seen her first at the road junction in town. Then once upstairs here in the zamin house on the night the intruder broke in. Alone several times … 'How do you know so much about everything!' she had remarked once in astonishment. 'You play the guitar, you research folk music … if you go on impressing me like this, I may fall in love with you.'

Marudamuthu was lamenting her fate and his. 'She told me not to come here tonight to sleep as I have been doing the past few nights. I should have come and protected her. Snehamma! Snehamma!' He broke down in tears and tried to stifle his sobs by holding his towel to his mouth.

They covered her body.

'Periasamy, be sure to tell the inspector about this in the morning.'

'Yes, ayya.'

'What is it, Thangarasu?'

'I don't know what to do. How will I break this news to her parents? What can I tell them? I'm feeling sick in the stomach with worry about that.'

'She suffered a deadly blow to the back of the head. Lost a lot of blood …'

Kalyanaraman stepped out of the room. 'Take it easy, ya!' spoke her familiar voice in his head. And then: 'You have disappointed me, Kalyanaraman. You should have used this opportunity to grab me and kiss me on the lips …'

Why did you come here, young woman? Why did you get yourself murdered?

What is it all about? What? What? Why did you have to go and die!!

As the light of dawn brushed the eastern sky, a crowd started collecting on the grounds of the zamindar's house. Ayyadurai seated himself on a chair on the verandah. The door to Snehalatha's room was shut, but the puppet doll was visible near her window. People were peeping into the room.

Periatha came running, wailing aloud and beating her chest. She started singing in a broken voice.

> '*In Aadhi Kailasam, the abode of Lord Siva,*
> *Aadhimoolam sat before Paramasiva*
> *Sorrowful in his mind that none were there,*
> *And turning to austerity …*'

'Hey, old woman. Keep quiet!' scolded Ayyadurai. 'Thangarasu, send for some gram flour to put …'

'Oh, you golden parrot! You precious life conceived after great austerity and prayer! You …'

'I told you to shut your mouth, woman!'

'Where is Periasamy?' someone wanted to know.

'He's gone to bring the inspector.'

'What about a cart to carry away the body? Will someone be bringing it?'

Ayyadurai came up to where Kalyanaraman was standing. He was holding a creased sheet of paper. 'Ayya, we have to prepare a report on this form. Can we talk in private?'

They moved away where they could not be overheard. 'Her body has to be sent to the town. Did you see anyone around?'

'I heard running footsteps …'

'When was that?'

'It must have been about one-thirty at night.'

'Hold on …' Ayyadurai scribbled on a piece of paper. 'At night ... around one o'clock … Ayya, could you write it yourself? You will do a good job of it …'

Kalyanaraman took the grubby, soiled paper from Ayyadurai. This was apparently the official form for reporting a suspicious death.

Zilla … Taluk … Village … Sent from the office of the magistrate to the … police station for investigation. This report is being sent to the official in charge.

Kalyanaraman's eyes ran through the page. It asked for all the material details. He started filling them in laboriously.

Name: Snehalatha

Male/Female: Female (He struck out 'Male'.)

Age: Approximately nineteen years

Colour of eyes: Black

Colour of hair: Black

Religious identity: None

Identifying marks: (Could he write 'A very sweet girl?' Then he remembered …) A small mole on the cheek

1. Time and place of discovery: 18 November 1978, one o'clock at night. Mempatti village. To whom was the body handed

over (cremation ground person, village official, etc.): Not yet

2. Wounds/injury marks found on the body: A severe wound on the back of the head, broken skull, heavy bleeding; an injury on the lip
3. If the wounds mentioned in point 2 above were made with a weapon or tool, what is it likely to be?: Do not know
4. Items sent with the body: Clothes (trousers and shirt), ornaments, glass bangles

Vomit: No

Weapons: No

Faeces: No

And thus was a lively, laughing, spirited young woman confined to a few lines on a grubby piece of official paperwork.

'Marudamuthu has gone to fetch the tractor. We can move her in an open trailer cart, right?'

That puppet in Snehalatha's room ... that voodoo doll with the darning needle thrust into its breast ... who could have put it there ...

Thangarasu came over and confided in Kalyanaraman. 'Ayya, I'm totally confused now. I don't know what to do.'

'Thangarasu, where do Snehalatha's parents live?'

'Somewhere in the north, ayya. I have the address.'

'Go to the telegraph office and send them a telegram immediately. I'll write it for you.'

'All right, I'll do that. For the past five or six days strange things have been happening here, ayya. All types of people come and go. And there's a thief who has been sneaking in on many nights ... Ennaya? What's the matter?'

This last remark was addressed to the man who was running up to them, looking dishevelled and distraught. It was Velli's father!

'Thangarasu, Velli is nowhere to be found.'

KARAIELLAM SHENBAGAPOO

14

'NOWHERE TO BE FOUND? What do you mean?'

'She went to take a bath this morning, but she's been missing after that. I've searched all over the village. Did Velli come here, ayya?'

'No, no, she didn't,' said Kalyanaraman. A new sense of dread crowded his mind and his thoughts swirled in eddies. Last night Snehalatha and Marudamuthu had left the villu paatu early, and Velli had followed them soon after. Obviously something must have happened afterwards.

'She did come home to sleep, didn't she?'

'I saw her early this morning,' said Velli's father. 'She told me she was going for a bath. Since she didn't come back home I went to the pipe where she usually bathes. Her pot was there, but there was no sign of Velli. Where could she have gone? My fear is …'

'Did you make proper enquiries in the village?'

'I've looked everywhere.'

'Maybe she is with that Marudamuthu fellow?' suggested Thangarasu.

'Not in this lifetime, ayya! She would never do that.'

'He has gone to fetch the tractor. We will ask him when he comes. He may know something. Meanwhile … Snehalatha's body is in her room. If you want to see …'

'I will take a quick look and then go and search for my daughter. Maybe she got scared and hid away somewhere. She is very timid by nature, saar.'

Velli's father peeped in through the window of Snehalatha's room. 'Tch tch!' he said and rushed away again in the quest to trace his missing daughter.

Kalyanaraman joined Ayyadurai, who was examining the rag puppet. 'I noticed it there last night itself,' he said. 'What is it?'

'It seems to be an *eval*.'

The word was unfamiliar to Kalyanaraman. 'Eval? What does that mean?'

'It's something people do to their enemies ... to those they don't like. They set an evil spirit to attack them,' explained Ayyadurai.

Periatha had an alternative theory about Snehalatha's death. 'Amman herself has killed her and sucked out all her blood. See how pale her body is ... white, like river sand. Oh, amma, amma! You beautiful sandalwood tree, you lovely jackfruit tree!'

'Ey, go far away over there!' he snapped at her. 'Sit there and weep.'

Periatha made her leisurely way towards the guava tree, stuffing fresh betel leaves into her mouth as she strolled along.

The tractor with a trailer attached made a noisy entrance into the grounds. Marudamuthu brought it to a halt and jumped out. Kalyanaraman noticed the man's reddened, swollen eyes; sure signs of grief.

'We can take her away, now, can't we?'

'Let the inspector come,' said Thangarasu. 'Someone has gone to bring him. I don't have the authority to move her.'

'Pah! What a delay! What if the man doesn't come?'

'Then we will see. But he will come.'

'Periasamy has gone on his bicycle to bring him,' said someone.

Kalyanaraman had been waiting for the first available opportunity to find out more about the events of the previous night. 'What happened last night, Marudamuthu?'

'Last night? Well, Snehamma got up in the middle of the villu paatu and told me she wanted to get back to her room. So I accompanied her to the zamindar's house and came back to the village.'

'You came back?'

'She said, "You may go now, Marudamuthu."'

He was looking down as he spoke, not meeting Kalyanaraman's face. *He is lying*, thought Kalyanaraman.

'Velli is missing. Did you know?'

Marudamuthu appeared shell-shocked. 'What … what …' he sputtered.

'Yes, her father came here looking for her. She has been missing since this morning. Have you seen her?'

'No, no I didn't see her. Missing …!'

Ayyadurai joined them. 'Yes, Marudu, everything is one big confusion. Velli has gone missing, and someone has cast an evil spirit on Snehalatha Amma here in her room. Did you see this doll?'

Marudamuthu took a close look at it. 'It must be from that pujari fellow. A few hard slaps on the face will make him spill the truth.'

'The inspector will take care of finding out about it.'

After a moment of thoughtful silence, Marudamuthu said, 'Ayyadurai, I'm beginning to have a certain suspicion.'

'I too have the same suspicion,' responded Ayyadurai promptly. Kalyanaraman was totally in the dark about what their suspicion could be.

'When the inspector comes, tell him frankly, Marudamuthu. Tell him everything. But still, it's so hard to imagine. Could it really be so …?'

'Why not? For the past few days she has been going around in some kind of frenzy. I was dreading what might happen if some evil spirit possessed her and drove her to do something terrible. And that is exactly what has happened.'

'Maybe that pujari fellow put her up to it.'

'No, not likely. Anyway, by the end of the day we will know. Three or four lashes from the inspector's belt will make that fellow spit out the truth.'

At ten o'clock the inspector arrived. He appeared to be about thirty-five years old. Both his uniform and his pencil moustache were neat, and the gold chain next to his mesh vest and the flashing ring with the insignia 'S' on his finger proclaimed the high status of the family into which he had married. He inspected the room and the body. When he had finished he did not seem to be particularly agitated about the situation. It could be that he had dealt with many murders earlier.

Kalyanaraman was introduced to the inspector: 'This is the ayya who found her.'

The inspector turned his attention to Kalyanaraman. He looked him up and down slowly, as though running him through a scanner.

'Your name?'

'Kalyanaraman.'

'When you found her was she still alive?'

'I can't be sure. The blood was still fresh.'

'Did she say anything? Any dying declaration?'

'No, nothing.'

'Are you related to her?'

'No.'

Ayyadurai intervened. 'I told you … she was the zamindar's granddaughter.'

'Hey, you keep quiet unless I ask you something.'

Having silenced Ayyadurai, the inspector continued his interrogation of Kalyanaraman.

'Was it you who wrote the death report?'

'Yes.'

'Ah, I thought so. The handwriting was not like what you would see in the village ... Periasamy, go and get me a packet of cigarettes.'

'Here you are,' said Kalyanaraman, holding out a cigarette to the inspector.

The inspector lit the cigarette and put an arm around Kalyanaraman's shoulder.

'Let's move away a little further where we can't be overheard.'

When they could talk in private, the inspector remarked, 'In this village, everyone has their own fanciful theories. Even before I got here I heard three separate versions of what happened. Some said that the ghost in the tamarind tree had struck her dead. Others claim that the pujari cast a spell to kill her. And then there is that missing girl with a name that means silver or brass or something. Ah, yes, Velli. One version is that this girl must be the murderer. There's no point asking those fellows for any reason or evidence for their theories. You are from the city, you're educated, what do you think happened?'

'It is definitely murder, sir. I saw the bloodstain trail starting right from her room.'

'Yes, so did I. When I lifted her head I could see the severe damage to the back of the skull. It was done there in that room. Then whoever it was tried to hide the crime by dragging the victim away towards the well. He heard someone coming, so he left her there and ran away.'

'I was the one he would have heard. I heard someone running away just before I got there.'

Marudamuthu approached them. 'Inspector Ayya, you should call that pujari fellow and question him.'

'There is a lot of talk in the village that the doll is the villain in this ...'

'There is something in that, saar ...'

'Yes, yes, it will be investigated. But first we must move the body to the town for the autopsy. Have the relatives been informed?'

Thangarasu nodded. 'Yes, I've sent a telegram to her parents.'

'Are you going to drive the tractor?' the inspector asked Marudamuthu.

'Yes, saar. That girl Velli is missing. I don't know what to think ...'

'Let us see to this woman first. Come, Kalyanaraman, let us move her body to the vehicle.' Snehalatha ... this was not Snehalatha. A blue hue had spread all over her skin; her mouth hung open, and a fly sat on the edge of her lip where the blood was now black and dry. Her beauty was gone. She was now just a piece of dead flesh that insects and other creatures would be waiting to feast upon ... Horrible!

'Come on, let's lift her,' urged the inspector. 'No one from the village will volunteer because they believe she was cursed to death. So it is you and me who will have to do it. Marudamuthu, you will help, right?'

As Snehalatha's body was brought out, Periatha started creating quite a racket with loud wailing that combined a bit of genuine fear with a lot of false grief.

'Ammaadi, ammaadi,
Even those assembled in the tahsildar's chamber
Will roll on the floor and weep.'

The tractor procession set out. Some people ran alongside; children climbed trees to get a good view; women covered their mouths with their hands as they watched. Kalyanaraman was in the trailer with Snehalatha's body, watching it bounce up and down in response to every bump on the road. Tears sprang to his eyes as though the sluices of a dam in his mind had been opened.

‘By the time the telegram reaches them and they arrive here, won’t it be very late?’ asked Thangarasu. And then, with concern in his voice, ‘Ayya, you’re crying.’

‘She was so vibrant … so full of life …’

‘Yes. By the time they cut her up and then sew her back, won’t it be very late before we can bring her back to the house? Today is the karagam day at the temple kodai festival. Advances have been paid to some important parties and people have gone to fetch them without knowing what’s been going on here.’

‘The tree spirit must have killed her,’ suggested someone.

‘Every time that Neeli story is told something happens. Even last year … do you remember … that child who died …?’

In Thirunilam town, in a building which was nothing more than a tile-roofed shed, the door of a room stood open. Snehalatha was brought in and laid on the raised cement slab in the centre of the room. The surgeon would get to her only after he had finished attending to his live patients. Meanwhile, they locked the door. Outside, many of the important people of Mempatti stood confused, not knowing what was going on. The inspector had slipped away at some point during these proceedings.

Kalyanaraman’s mind felt battered. He moved some distance away and lit a cigarette. The whole period, from the time he had first met Snehalatha up to the moment the shed door was shut, seemed like a hallucination. In one corner of his mind, the question, ‘Why is Velli missing?’ kept repeating itself … with no answers. Maybe she had gone on a visit to a neighbouring village and had returned home by now? But no! Why would she just leave her water pot at the bathing place and go to the next village without telling her father about it? Or, could it be that she … no, no, che … stop it!

Her father didn't seem to be among the crowd outside. He was probably still looking for his daughter, still asking every passer-by, 'Have you seen Velli? She has been missing since this morning ...'

Where are you, Velli?

'They're selling ladies' fingers for just a rupee,' remarked Periasamy. He set off with a bag.

Kalyanaraman looked at the locked door behind which the dead Snehalatha lay. No one seemed to have any sense of urgency about her any longer. Each of them took off on their separate errands. Thangarasu, probably deciding that his duty was done once he had sent off the telegram, went away to buy a length of cloth he needed. Ayyadurai had stepped into a barber's salon, taken off his banian and raised both arms to have his armpits shaved.

'They may take her away only tomorrow morning,' said someone. The crowd melted away. Soon Kalyanaraman realized he was the only one still there in front of the locked door.

In his mind he played a few notes on his Malvina guitar; Snehalatha swayed to the music, gently, gracefully, beautifully. He heard her voice. 'My brothers called me "Snake".'

Young woman, where were you born, where did you grow up, what are the dreams that you kept locked in your mind? And after all that you end up like this. In Thirunilam in a dark blue karuneelam condition to undergo postmortem! His heart swelled with deep pity at her plight.

Marudamuthu came over and sat on the ground near Kalyanaraman.

'What a lively woman she was, ayya! She told me, "If you had got some education you could have become an important man, a collector." This towel of mine still has a hint of her scent. So clever she was! And how well she spoke! Her grace, her manner, everything ... che!' Marudamuthu widened his eyes and blinked in an effort to hold back his tears.

'Marudamuthu, I'm terrified at the thought that the same thing could have happened to Velli.'

'I'm not. I strongly suspect she has done this murder and gone into hiding.'

'Che, che, che!' protested Kalyanaraman.

'You are saying "che che" because you don't know what happened last night.'

'Last night? What happened?'

Marudamuthu hesitated for a moment before speaking. 'I think she flew into a jealous rage when she saw Snehalatha and me together.'

'Oh, so you did see Velli last night?'

'Forget it now, ayya. Anyway everything will come out in the investigation. How long can she hide, the slander-mongering wretch! I'll find her, see if I don't! Where can you hide from me, di? Ayya, I know all the places she goes to, anywhere she may have hidden. She often goes to the *pachai kulam*; there's a mandapam there. Or maybe she went to her mother's place in Mevalapuram. Then she has a cousin, her aunt's daughter, who is working in a school in town. She could be there. Anyway, she can hide like this for two days at most. Then she has to get back. Am I right? What do you say?'

'But why should she hide at all?'

'Oh, what a question, ayya!'

'Marudamuthu, when do you plan to go back to Mempatti?'

'Why do you ask?'

'It looks as if nothing is going to happen here till the evening at least.'

'However long it takes I will stay till Snehamma's parents get here. That is my duty. I won't eat or drink anything before that.'

'I feel rather unwell after staying awake the whole of last night. I will go back to my room and rest now and come back in the evening.'

'All right, ayya. Shall I hire a bicycle for you?'

Slowly and wearily Kalyanaraman pedalled back to Mempatti. The village was virtually bare of life. There was no one near the peepul tree in the village square. The temple was locked. For the first time, the mandapam held no sight or sound of a living thing … except the dog Mani which seemed to be aimlessly moving around, maybe searching for someone …

When he got to the zamin mansion Kalyanaraman went into his room and collapsed onto his bed right away, without bothering to undress. He was half asleep when he felt someone touching his feet. He woke with a start and sat up.

Velli!

15

Velli looked exhausted. She was covered in dirt, her hair matted with mud and a few dried leaves, a livid red scratch across her cheek, and intense terror in her eyes. The pottu had been wiped off her forehead, and her lips were dry and cracked. She was panting and heaving like a dying bird with a fluttering heart.

'Velli! What happened?'

She looked around nervously and spoke in a faint, feeble voice. 'Ayya, will you protect me?'

'What do you mean, Velli? Everyone is looking for you.'

Velli started sobbing and wailing. 'Don't hand me over to the police, ayya. Save me. Tell me a way out. I had to get here secretly, hiding here and there on the way. I didn't know what I was doing when I carried out that deed. I wasn't thinking ... I'm so scared ...'

'Wait, wait! What deed are you talking about? What did you do?'

'I killed that woman, ayya.'

'My God! You ... you wretch!' Kalyanaraman stared at her disbelievingly. 'You? You did that?'

'Ayya, don't hand me over. Show me a way to save myself. I'm begging you ...' Velli stooped to touch his feet.

Kalyanaraman moved away. 'Enough of all that. Stand up.'

'They'll send me to jail and hang me by my neck. They will watch and laugh when my arms and legs start twitching while I slowly die. Oh, amma ... ammadi ...what can I do?'

'Wait! Stop ranting and raving.'

She grabbed his hands and raised them reverentially to her eyes. 'Don't tell them, ayya. I didn't do it deliberately. I didn't know what I was doing ...'

'Velli, did you attack Snehalatha?'

'Yes.'

'My God! You sinful creature! Why did you do it?'

A jumble of confusing thoughts popped up in Kalyanaraman's mind. What was he to do with this girl? Should he try to hide her? Or should he simply hand her over to the authorities?

He looked at her again. The sari folds on her chest were wet with her tears. Her forehead was furrowed with fear. She blew her nose and then slid down to the floor. She sat on her haunches, held her bent head in her hands and wailed. 'Oh God! God!'

'Where were you all day?'

'I was hiding in the woods . . . Karuppan *kadu* ... right from the morning. After it started getting dark I came here to beg you to ... you are the only one I trust, ayya ... I can't depend on anyone else. Please save me. It's all my wretched fate! I don't know what came over me. I didn't do it on purpose. I'm so scared ...!'

'Look here, there's no use wailing now. Tell me exactly what happened and I'll try to help you as much as I can.'

'So you'll save me? You'll protect me, ayya?'

'Stop rambling, you wretched girl! Just say what happened.'

'Don't hit me, ayya. Please! I'm a motherless girl.' Again a bout of sobbing and a flood of tears.

He waited for her to finish weeping. He realized that she was in an extremely fragile state of mind, consumed by guilt, anxiety and fear. *Kalyanaraman*, he told himself, *Here is a test for you. You can either play safe, hand her over and finish all this with the least fuss; or you can stick your neck out and risk trouble down the line. If you really love Velli, you will protect her. But you are hesitant, afraid. Yours is a fair-weather love. Topmost in your mind is the concern for your own safety and well-being. This love of yours cannot face obstacles and challenges; it is a boat that can sail only on calm waters. Yet, in such a crisis, what has love got to do with it? Isn't my future, my fate, the most important thing now? Leave me alone, girl. So that's it? Yes, who am I after all? An outsider. I've been caught against my will in a tangled web of mystery. If I help this girl, I will definitely be in deep trouble. This is murder, no less. And yet … yet …*

He looked at Velli. She blew her nose and started talking. The words spilled out of her. 'Ayya, I saw the two of them leaving in the middle of the villu paatu. First she and then Marudamuthu. I followed them. They came here, went into her room and turned off the light. Right from childhood I have worshipped that man. He was the one I was going to marry. I was boiling with fury. I started shouting from where I stood outside: "All my life I've never thought of any man but you. How can you do this to me? Will you not suffer for this?"

'He came out and threw a stone at me. "Shut up, you bitch!" he shouted. I went home crying. I lay down, but my whole body was burning with every breath I took. The sounds of the villu paatu were going on. I was reminded of Neeli's story. She did not spare those who did harm to her. She chased them through several lifetimes till she got her revenge. At that moment Isakki Amman appeared before me. "Why are you cringing and crying like this? Go and kill that Moodevi and drink her blood." Isakki Amman possessed me. It was not I who decided to go back that night to the zamin house, it was Isakki Amman who made me walk there. I strode boldly without any hesitation or fear. On the way I picked up a stone by the wayside. When I reached the place, that woman was sitting in the moonlight just outside the door to her room. "You wretch!" I cried out. "You have ruined my life!" I raised the stone and threw it at her head.'

'Oh, no … no!'

'It wasn't me, ayya, it was Isakki Amman who did it. Pazhayanur Neeli did it.'

'Don't talk rubbish. Look here, Velli, what you did was a serious crime. Do you realize that?'

'I didn't think she would die, ayya. I didn't even look at her again. I came straight back home. Only the next morning when I went for my bath I heard she was dead. Yes, I did what I did, but it was all dictated by Amman. So she did it, not me.'

'Velli, no one will swallow your explanation about Amman. You acted out of jealousy.'

'Not jealousy, ayya. It was love. My love for that traitor, may he rot in hell. Yet, even now, my foolish heart speaks only his name. Listen, someone's coming! Ayya, please don't give me up. Please save me.' They could hear some people approaching, talking as they came. Velli's eyes pleaded along with her words. She was like a bird fluttering desperately in the sparks from a flame. After a moment of indecision, Kalyanaraman sprang into action. He moved the cupboard at the end of the room and opened the hidden door behind it, the one in which he had discovered a jumble of things and that precious diary. 'Hurry!' he urged Velli. 'Go and hide in that room. Stay absolutely silent till I come and fetch you.'

He hurriedly pushed her into the storage room, shut the door and dragged the cupboard back over it.

The inspector, Constable Periasamy and Ayyadurai came into Kalyanaraman's room. 'Appaada!' grunted Ayyadurai, mopping his face with his towel and sitting down.

'What happened? Did the parents arrive?'

'No, no news from them. It looks like tomorrow is the earliest they can do something about the body.'

'Where's Marudamuthu?'

'He is searching for Velli.'

'Why is he searching for her?'

'Everyone is looking for her. Someone has been sent to Mevalapur to see if she's there.'

The inspector spoke for the first time. 'Mr Kalyanaraman, when was the last time you saw Velli?'

'Velli? Why do you ask?'

Ayyadurai explained. 'It seems likely that she is the one who killed Snehalatha. All the signs point to her.'

'Periasamy,' said the inspector, 'go and fetch that pujari fellow. The truth will come out, Ayyadurai ... Mr Kalyanaraman ... you will see ... Marudamuthu told me the whole background. He said that just because he was spending time with the zamin's granddaughter Snehalatha to show her around and help her, Velli had misunderstood them and become jealous and angry. He says you were also there when she lost her temper and ranted and raved at him about it. What do you think, Mr Kalyanaraman?'

Then, switching to English, the inspector asked, 'What sort of girl is Velli? Is she the type who would be capable of killing someone out of jealousy?'

Kalyanaraman was startled by such a question. What should he say? 'I didn't think so, but I could be wrong. It's not a simple thing to gauge a woman's mind and the depth of her feelings.'

'If you were to compare Velli and Snehalatha, who would you say was the stronger of the two?'

'Rather than strength of body, you should be thinking about strength of mind,' suggested Kalyanaraman. 'What did the autopsy show?'

'A severe blow to the back of the head. Internal bleeding in the brain. Take a look at this piece from a bangle.' The inspector held out a broken piece of a green bangle. 'Both Velli's father and Marudamuthu identified it as a piece from a bangle that Velli was wearing. It was found in the doorway of Snehalatha's room. It shows Velli was here last night.'

'It could be from some earlier visit ...'

'No, because her friends have told us that Velli bought bangles like these at the market yesterday evening. Most importantly, why is she hiding?'

'Why ...?' ventured Kalyanaraman hesitantly.

'We will find her, never fear. It's an open-and-shut case.'

Periasamy entered.

'Periasamy, where is that pujari?'

The pujari, in an undervest, came in with slow, reluctant steps. He had taught his eyes to convey religious fervour, but today they had forgotten the lesson; instead they openly displayed his sly and dishonest nature. He looked at the inspector and tried to put on an ingratiating smile.

'Periasamy,' ordered the inspector, 'fetch that doll. *Yo*, Pujari, do you remember this?'

The pujari looked at the voodoo puppet and the veins in his forehead bulged.

'I remember,' he muttered.

'What is it?'

'It's the doll on which I cast a spell and gave to Velli as she wanted.'

'Why did she want it?'

'No particular reason.'

With no warning, the inspector brought his knee up sharply, thudding into the pujari's abdomen. '*Ayemma!*' grunted the pujari, staggering backwards. 'Please don't hit me.'

'Don't lie to me. I'll give you a thrashing with my belt. What did you tell Velli when you gave her this doll?'

The pujari sat doubled up against the wall, massaging his bruised stomach. As for the inspector, having vented some of his accumulated frustration of that long, wearying day, a day of murder and autopsy and interviews, he was now calmer.

'Speak, pujari. If you tell the truth I'll let you go.'

'I swear on Amman, Ayya. Velli came to me and said, "Pujari, that woman is a witch. I must finish her off somehow." I took an offering from her, gave her that doll and cast a spell upon some vibhuti. I gave the things to her and said, "Go to her room, leave these near her and come away." That's all I did. Was that wrong?'

'Pujari, what did she tell you about the zamindar's granddaughter?'

'She wanted to kill her. She asked me for poison to do the job. But I told her that she should just try to chase her away from here, not kill her. That's why I cast the spell.'

'You're the first one who needs to be chased away from here. You have been deceiving and cheating everyone. Why is the doll's body pierced with this darning needle?'

The pujari explained hesitantly, 'If the doll is pierced like this and a spell is cast, then the victim will feel sharp pains in her stomach.'

'How much money did you take from Velli for this?'

'Not much, saar. Inspector Ayya, if I had even dreamt that she would go and do something like this, I would have advised her and stopped her. I do these magic spells only to earn a livelihood, ayya. I have six children, all daughters. With my temple salary I can't …' There were tears of fear in the pujari's eyes.

'All right, go and stand over there. Stop crying like a woman!'

'The temple kodai festival has come to a standstill,' remarked Ayyadurai.

'Do you have a cigarette?' asked the inspector. Kalyanaraman gave him a cigarette and lit it for him.

'If the girl has left the village, where could she have gone?' wondered the inspector. 'Only two trains stop at Thirunilam station. Everyone at the station knows her and they say she did not come there today. If she had gone to the bus stand, the people at the tea stall opposite would have noticed her. But nothing there either. So she must have walked. She couldn't have walked very far. So she could be hiding right here in the village. What do you say, Ayyadurai?'

'She is not in the village, saar. Every possible place has been searched … the well, the lakeside, Karuppan *thottam* … everywhere. She's certainly left the village.'

'Have you searched this zamin house?'

Ayyadurai appeared surprised. 'No, saar, we haven't searched this house yet.'

'Periasamy, conduct a thorough search of this house. There must be plenty of hiding places here.'

Ayyadurai said, 'Ayya, even now some people in the village are convinced that the zamin's granddaughter was killed by someone casting a spell.'

'Spell ... pell ... mell … all rubbish! Come, ya! Let's take a look around. Do you have a flashlight?'

'No, ayya.'

'Kalyanaraman, do you have a torch?'

The inspector and Periasamy set off on their tour of the house with Kalyanaraman's torch to light the way. The pujari asked, 'Now what about me?'

'Come back here tomorrow,' ordered Ayyadurai. 'Inspector Ayya is going to conduct an enquiry.'

The footsteps of the search party moving around upstairs drifted down faintly. 'They will finish searching upstairs, and then they will return to this room; then they will move that cupboard and open that door; and then …'

'I've had nothing but a bit of coffee since this morning,' said Ayyadurai.

A new worry assailed Kalyanaraman. *Velli must be very hungry*, he thought.

Soon the inspector and Periasamy returned from their search. 'Most of the rooms upstairs are locked from the outside,' said the inspector. His gaze swept around Kalyanaraman's room. 'What's in that cupboard?' he asked.

16

KALYANARAMAN'S HEART WAS POUNDING. Periasamy walked up to the cupboard and opened it. 'Oh, God!' groaned Kalyanaraman inwardly. 'If he decides to pull the cupboard away and open the door behind it, Velli will be discovered. My fate will be sealed then and there. I will be an accessory to murder.'

The next moment he felt a twinge of guilt that his first concern had been for his own safety. 'Poor Velli, poor girl!' he reminded himself.

Periasamy noticed that there was a door behind the cupboard. 'Where does this door lead, ayya?'

'I don't know. Is there a door there? I didn't know that.'

'Yes, come and look.'

Kalyanaraman went and looked. 'It must be one of the many rooms that have been locked. I haven't been in there.'

'Why don't you go inside and take a look just in case, Periasamy,' suggested the inspector.

Kalyanaraman's limbs trembled. *Velli? Have you hidden yourself properly inside?*

'All right, saar. Will you also come?' The question was directed at Kalyanaraman.

'Why? Are you afraid of something? A brave constable you are! Come, Periasamy, let's inspect the room,' offered Kalyanaraman. The door opened with a protesting creak. In the pitch darkness inside, Kalyanaraman's torch beam picked up random objects, while his heart sent up a fervent prayer that it should not reveal Velli's face anywhere.

'Who is going to come into a place like this?' commented Kalyanaraman. 'Also, someone would have had to come through my room to get here.'

'Inspector saar has this theory about it. I'm trying to tell him it is the work of an evil spirit, but he doesn't listen. I know Velli well. She couldn't have done something like this. She doesn't have the courage and strength to do it. The inspector refuses to accept that.'

As Periasamy was voicing his complaint about the inspector, Kalyanaraman's torch beam picked up a fold of sari peeping out from behind a cupboard. He quickly turned the light away. At that moment Periasamy was seized by a fit of sneezing. He had seen nothing.

They emerged from the room. 'There's no one in there, saar,' reported Periasamy. A bicycle bell announced the arrival of Thangarasu. He appeared hurried and somewhat agitated.

'Is the inspector saar here?' he gasped out, even as he entered the room.

The inspector stepped forward. 'I'm here. What's the matter, Thangarasu?'

'Please look at this telegram. They gave it to me in the town and asked me to read it, but I couldn't understand what it says.'

The inspector took the telegram, read it, and looked meaningfully at Kalyanaraman. 'When did this arrive?' he asked Thangarasu.

'This evening. The messenger seems to have come here and found no one, so he went back to the town with it. I got it at about seven o'clock and brought it here at once.'

'What's this? A new twist …' The inspector handed the telegram to Kalyanaraman.

'*Thangarasu Mempatti Panchayat your telegram recd. There is no Snehalatha in our family. All our daughters are alive. T.V. Raja.*'

Kalyanaraman raised his eyes from the telegram's startling news. 'Thangarasu, explain this. Didn't you say these people are her parents?'

The inspector cut in. 'Who is this T.V. Raja?'

'He is the chinna zamindar ... the old zamindar's younger son. Snehalatha said she was the daughter of this chinna zamindar. That's why I gave that address. This ayya is the one who wrote it out for me to send.'

'What did you say in the telegram?' the inspector asked Kalyanaraman.

'I wrote, "Your daughter Snehalatha has met with untimely death. Come at once."'

'And now he has replied asking "Snehalatha? Who's she?" Ey, Thangarasu, what's all this?'

Thangarasu, confused and totally embarrassed, stood rubbing his hands together. He looked at the inspector nervously.

'How did you decide that she was the zamindar's granddaughter?' asked the inspector.

'I didn't decide, saar. She herself told me.'

'When did she tell you that?'

'As soon as she arrived. She came the day after this ayya arrived, quite unexpectedly ... very modern in pants and shirt, and she addressed me by name. "Thangarasu!" she called me. She mentioned the names of the older zamindar and the chinna zamindar correctly. She said her father, the chinna zamindar, had sent her to spend a few days at the zamin house. "He wrote to you," she told me, "didn't you get my father's letter?" When she said all this correctly, and even the names of the other members of the family including the children, I naturally believed her. In fact, there was never any doubt in my mind and so the question of believing her or not never arose. So who was she?'

'My goodness! Another new headache!' The inspector looked at Kalyanaraman. 'What can I hope to investigate in this wretched village? Half the people are convinced that a ghost killed her. And that girl Velli has gone missing. There is circumstantial evidence against her for the murder. I'm convinced she is in hiding somewhere. And now it turns out that the murdered woman was not the zamindar's granddaughter! So now we don't know who the murderer was and we also don't know who the victim was! Wonderful! Ey, you stupid fellow, someone comes to you out of the blue and spins a tale and you immediately open up the house for her. But I suppose I can't blame you. You would have been dazzled by her. You'd have been ready to open up the treasury for her if you could. Don't I know you well! Who is your woman in Thirunilam? Is it Jameela?'

'Saar … what, saar!'

'She spoke about a letter. Did a letter ever arrive?'

'No.'

'Shouldn't that have made you suspicious?'

'Yes … that's true …'

'What do you mean, yes? What did I ask you?'

Thangarasu was baffled. He stood tongue-tied.

Speaking in English to Kalyanaraman, the inspector said, 'I think this fellow may himself have abetted this crime.'

'I don't think so.'

'What's your opinion?'

'It's very confusing. I was sure all along that Snehalatha was not everything she pretended to be. I could sense that she was here with a particular plan. I even confronted her with that accusation once, but she just laughed it off. Inspector, you should talk to Marudamuthu. He spent a lot of time with Snehalatha. In fact that is why Velli became jealous. They were always meeting and talking.'

'Particular plan? What plan?'

'I don't know.' Even as he said the words, the images of Ratnavathy's diary and the pressed champaka flower between its pages rose in his mind. *I won't mention those things now*, he told himself. *Let the inspector talk to Marudamuthu and find out what he can. Everything I know is only secondhand. Even if I don't know who*

Snehalatha really was, I and only I know for sure that Velli killed Snehalatha. That's a piece of knowledge that's sticking in my throat; I can neither swallow it nor spit it out. It's making me sick. What can I do with that girl? How many days can I keep her shut up in a dark room? How many days can I keep lying to people?

'Where is Marudamuthu?' asked the inspector.

Thangarasu said, 'He's still out looking for Velli. He said he would come here soon. What will you do with Snehalatha's body?'

'Once Ayyadurai comes we will get the death report corrected. "Corpse of person of unknown parentage, unknown identity" … that's what we must write. Ayyayyo! What a muddle!'

Kalyanaraman hardly took in the conversation going on around him. He was reliving recent images and memories. *Who are you, Snehalatha?*

Bits and pieces of conversations and interactions involving Snehalatha swirled and formed a shifting collage in his mind. That night when she arrived … sounds from upstairs … chairs being shifted, footsteps. A shadowy figure leaping from the parapet. 'Folk music? Whom are you trying to fool? Tell me the real reason you're here.' An old diary. 'Have you finished reading it?' 'Not yet.' Snehalatha locking the diary in her suitcase. Her smirk as she said, 'Marudamuthu and I are going to a secret place', and Marudamuthu's foolish grin as he added, 'Yes, we are going to pick flowers, champaka flowers.' The two of them laughing together, delighting in their shared secret … Then, just the previous night, why had Marudamuthu brought a coil of thick rope?

'Inspector, if you question Marudamuthu the whole story will come out.'

'What story?'

'The real story. Who Snehalatha was and why she came here.'

'The priority now is to find that girl Velli. I have hardly slept for two nights in a row. Last night they said the minister was coming and so I was on duty.'

The inspector, Ayyadurai and Periasamy left together. Kalyanaraman waited two minutes after the sound of their voices died away in the distance. He bolted the door to his room from the inside, hurried to the cupboard and pushed it aside. He opened the door, stepped in and nervously called out 'Velli!'

Silence.

'Velli, don't be afraid. They have gone away. You can come out safely now.'

Still, no response.

He shone the torch beam at the spot where he had seen a fold of her sari earlier. He walked softly to the cupboard and looked behind it. Velli was there, hand on her chest, terror in her eyes, stone-still as though stuck in that corner with glue.

'Velli, there's no one here. Come out. I need to talk to you.'

Very slowly, still fearful, she emerged from behind the cupboard.

'Ayya, you didn't tell them about me?'

'No.'

Her eyes expressed her gratitude. 'What if they come back?'

'They won't. Come out of this room with me. If anyone comes, you can always hide here again.'

She dusted off the cobwebs from her hair and clothes and followed Kalyanaraman out of the hidden room. She sneezed once. Her clothes were stuck to her body with sweat, and the shape of her bosom was clearly visible. That didn't seem to bother her. Her eyes still held the look of a trapped bird.

'What did the police say?'

'They are all looking for you.'

'What a lot of trouble I am causing you, ayya! Can you somehow smuggle me out and take me to my father?'

'Your father? That's the first place the police will be keeping an eye on.'

'Then what can I do? My father will feel tortured with worry about me. I've never been parted from him even for a day. What lies the pujari said about me! He claimed that I asked him for poison! He was the one who asked me to bring a chicken to offer as a sacrifice and suggested casting a spell. I paid him twenty-five rupees plus some change.'

'What for?'

'He said he would make a doll and cast a spell on it and pierce a needle through its body, and also give me some magic vibhuti. He said if I put the doll in her room and sprinkle the vibhuti on her doorstep, her clothes would catch fire. I did that and waited, but nothing happened. Only after that did Amman possess me and lead me here to attack that woman.'

'Look here, Velli, give up this talk of Amman guiding you and a spirit possessing you. No court will accept such an argument.'

'But that is the truth, ayya,' she insisted in all sincerity. It was very evident that she was truly convinced about it.

'Oh, God! What am I going to do with you!'

'If I'm a problem for you, ayya, I'll go away.' Tears had sprung to her eyes.

'Wait! Hold on! Do you realize what a dangerous situation I have put myself into by hiding you here? I've become your partner in crime.'

'That's why I'm telling you I'll go.'

'Where will you go?'

'To him.'

'You mean Marudamuthu? He's been searching for you high and low.'

Her face brightened. 'Really? He's searching for me?'

'Yes. To hand you over to the police.'

'Che, that can't be. He won't stab me in the back like that.'

'Why are you still pining for that fellow after all this?'

'I did this only for him, saar. That evil monster woman had trapped him in her clutches. She was poisoning him slowly. I wanted to release him. That's why Amman made me pick up that stone and …'

'Again Amman! You stupid, stupid girl!'

'Please don't scold me, ayya!' She fell at his feet. His mind told her, *Don't fall at my feet, fall on me*. All kinds of schemes and ploys crossed his mind rapidly. He could sleep with Velli tonight and hand her over to the police in the morning. Or, under cover of darkness he could somehow smuggle her to Madras, change her name, cut her hair, change her appearance, teach her English … won't work!

'Velli, the very first time I saw you, I liked you. That's why I'm helping you now.'

'You're a god, ayya!'

'*Chut!* I don't want to be divine, Velli.'

How could he signal his feelings to her? 'Velli, if I help you, will you …'

'We both will forever be grateful to you, ayya. We will slave and work ourselves to the bone for you.'

'Who both? You and Marudamuthu?'

'Yes, ayya.'

'What an idiot you are! He is feverishly looking for you everywhere just to hand you over. And you are …'

'He will never betray me, saar. Just wait and see. Once the madness from her poison goes away, he will come to me and say, "Velli, Velli! My darling! I have treated you badly, pilla. Please forgive me."'

'Then why did you ever come to me? You could have gone straight to him.'

'I don't know why I came here, ayya.'

'Curse my fate!' exclaimed Kalyanaraman in frustration, slapping himself on the forehead.

'He is just silly, saar. Empty-headed. He just ran after her blindly, but in his heart he still loves me. If I had gone to him, I wouldn't be able to tell him, "Do this or do that to save me." He wouldn't think of a plan. That's why I came to you.'

Kalyanaraman was seething with fury. On top of his weariness and his own inner demons torturing him with uncertainty and making him question his own lack of integrity, now here was Velli declaring that she had used him as a convenience!

'Have you eaten anything?' he asked roughly.

'No, ayya.'

He picked up a loaf of bread from the table, tore it in half and handed it to her along with some sugar. 'Eat!' he ordered. She took the bread and bit into it reluctantly. She raised her head and glanced out through the window. The moment she set eyes on the door of Snehalatha's room, her whole body was racked by heaving sobs.

'What now?'

'I would never kill even an ant, saar. Where did my aggressiveness come from? It was all for the sake of this wretched man.' She shot verbal arrows at the absent Marudamuthu. 'Are you still pining for that woman? Don't you realize my worth?'

'Akka! So you're here!' The shout from the window startled Kalyanaraman. He swung around. It was Velli's brother Rajavelu.

'Rajavelu! What ... what are you doing here?' asked Kalyanaraman.

'Akka, the whole village is looking for you. Marudamuthu Annan said if anyone sees you he must be told at once. I'll run and tell him now and come back.'

'Wait, wait! Stop! Don't do that!'

But it was too late. The boy was headed fast towards the village. The *drrr* sound of his imaginary tractor faded into the distance.

17

KALYANARAMAN GLARED ANGRILY AT the retreating figure of Rajavelu.

'That stupid boy is going to spread the news all over the village that he saw me here. What can I do now?' asked Velli in agitation.

'Velli, you must go and hide in that same place again. There's nothing else we can do. I'll try to handle it.'

'What if they come and search that room again?'

'Then you'll get caught. That's it.' Kalyanaraman's pent-up irritation was now bursting its bounds.

'Shall I run away?'

'Don't talk nonsense! Where can you run. You will get caught at once. Just do as I tell you, go and hide in that room.'

'I'm afraid they'll find me …' Her wide eyes, filled with fear, looked at him pleadingly.

A new idea struck him. 'Velli, come up close to me,' he said. When she stepped up near him, he took her hands and inspected her nails.

'Scratch my arm with your nails,' he ordered her. 'When those people come, I must convince them that I tried to restrain you, but that you scratched me, wriggled out of my grasp and fled. Come along … scratch me!'

Velli hesitated. 'No, ayya, I can't … I won't do that.' She retreated a few steps.

Kalyanaraman grabbed hold of her and locked her in a close embrace.

‘Let me go! Leave me!’ She struggled; she panted and pleaded. Then … she scratched his arm in desperation. Immediately he released her and inspected his arm.

‘Yes, this will do. This is what I wanted. Now go and hide in that room and let me manage everything else.’

As the realization of his plan dawned on her, Velli was overcome with gratitude. ‘Ayya, I don’t know how to thank you ...’

‘There’s no time for that now. Run! Run and hide!’

She disappeared into the secret room behind the cupboard. Kalyanaraman stood still for a while, collecting his thoughts. Her desperation had made the scratches very convincing. Bright red lines of blood were appearing on his arm.

Sounds of approaching footsteps … Kalyanaraman looked through the window. Hurricane lanterns, lamps and flashlights wove patterns in the darkness of the night.

Out in front of the group was Marudamuthu, followed closely by Velli’s brother. Next came Thangarasu and Periasamy. The inspector was not far behind. His voice could be heard giving orders.

‘Where is she?’ demanded Marudamuthu as he burst into Kalyanaraman’s room.

‘Who?’

‘Velli.’

‘She ran away,’ said Kalyanaraman, looking at his scratched arm. ‘A regular wild beast, that girl! The way she struggled … look, she scratched me like a wildcat!’

‘She ran away? Which way did she go?’

‘From what I saw, she seemed to be running towards the village. I was trying to talk to her to make her calm down and see reason. I was making progress, but just then that silly Rajavelu fellow shouted “Akka!” through the window. Immediately she became tense again and tried to run away. I caught and held her, but she scratched my arm, struggled free and ran away.’

'You let her get away?'

'What more could I have done, Marudamuthu? How could I have stopped her?'

'What are you saying, ayya? You knew this girl is a murderess. She is a mere girl. Couldn't you have restrained her? A slap on the ear or a cut on the nape of the neck would have done the job. What kind of man are you?'

'Marudamuthu, why are you still talking? Let's go,' said Thangarasu.

'Che!' snorted Marudamuthu in disgust. 'Come along, she can't have gone far. Thangarasu, you look near the canal; Periasamy, search in the village. I will go along the lane to the woods.'

Just then the inspector entered the room. 'Ennayya? What's happening here?'

'She's been allowed to escape,' Marudamuthu informed him.

'What!'

'Yes. Ayya allowed her to escape. Ayya, she murdered an unsuspecting woman by smashing a stone on her head ... and you let her get away!'

'How could I know that? So far the talk was that she could be a suspect, that's all.'

Kalyanaraman could feel the inspector's eyes drilling into him. He avoided looking at him. Instead, he urged the others, 'Hurry, go and look for her. Don't waste any more time.'

'Hold on!' the inspector said. He turned towards Velli's brother. '*Ey le*, come here. What's your name?'

'Rajavelu.'

'Tell me, Rajavelu, when you came here where was your sister?'

'She was sitting and talking with this ayya.'

'Were they fighting?'

'Mm ... hm, no.'

'What did you see?'

'I saw akka coming out of a room there at the back.'

'And did ayya grab her, pull her, hit her?'

'Che, che, no. Ayya is a very nice man. He only asked how she was, and then they were chatting.'

'What's all this, Mr Kalyanaraman?' asked the inspector sternly. Marudamuthu interrupted indignantly. 'Oh, so that's the story! Chatting, were you?' He grabbed Kalyanaraman's arm aggressively. 'So, where's she?'

'Look, I'm telling the truth. She scratched me on my arm and ran away. Look at the blood on my arm.'

'They have both committed the crime together!' declared Marudamuthu.

'What nonsense are you talking?'

'This ayya, this nice Brahmin ayya is the one who hid Velli when we were all searching for her. Together they murdered Snehamma … look at his face! See how he is staring guiltily!'

'Come, let's give him a thrashing.'

The inspector tried to intervene. 'Hold on … hold on, da.'

But they were in no mood to listen. They strode menacingly towards Kalyanaraman. His mind was racing, his heart was thudding, his hair stood on end, his whole body trembled. 'AYYO!' Marudamuthu's first blow landed on Kalyanaraman's hip. Unbearable pain spread like wildfire through his body. 'Kkk,' he choked and coughed.

'Don't! Wait! Marudamuthu, stop.' More hands were raised against him. 'Inspector, why are you silently watching this?'

'Dei, hold on for a moment, da,' said the inspector. The raised hands froze mid-air. 'Periasamy, go and look properly inside that room. If he has hidden Velli, she must be in there. Look here, Mr Kalyanaraman, if I find that you have been lying to me or misleading me, I won't be responsible for the thrashing you will get from these fellows. All of you, wait. We will search the whole house. Periasamy and Marudamuthu, go and look in that room first.'

The cupboard was moved aside. The door was opened. The two of them entered with lanterns. Thangarasu, the boy Rajavelu and a couple of other men also crowded into the room.

'No, no!' shouted Kalyanaraman desperately. 'There's no one there! Listen to me. There's no one.' A dark veil was being drawn across his eyes. They would march her out into the centre of his room ... and then ... what would their bloodlust make them do? *But surely the inspector wouldn't just be a silent spectator. No, maybe not; he would just move away outside so that he need not witness anything. Then one after the other they would ... no, no, NO! Velli, I'm so sorry. It's because of me that you got caught like this...*

Marudamuthu emerged from the room, and then Periasamy. The others followed. Everyone who had gone in came out. No Velli!

'Ennayya?' asked the inspector.

'She's not in there.' Marudamuthu's head was bowed in evident disappointment.

'Not there? Did you search properly?'

'Yes, yes. Every inch, every particle. Nobody there.'

Kalyanaraman's relief overshadowed everything else at that moment. He didn't care how it had happened, it was enough that it had indeed happened. He even forgot the pain of the blow he had received.

'You see? I told you, didn't I? And you accused me. Me! Go and search the whole house. Search as much as you want. You started thrashing me. Hah! Brave fellows! Eight of you piling up on me!'

'Search the other parts of the house anyway, Periasamy,' advised the inspector.

'Yes, do that. You fellows didn't believe me. You decided I had hidden her in that room. By now she would have run at least four miles. What energy she has, that girl! How fast she can run!'

'Come, da, let's search the house.'

'Sit down, Mr Kalyanaraman,' said the inspector soothingly. 'You have been injured by those rough fellows. That's the trouble with people like that. Suddenly they lose control and start behaving violently.'

'But still, I'm surprised that you just stood there and watched passively, inspector.'

'What do you mean? I'm the one who stopped them. I saved your life, do you realize that?'

Kalyanaraman shot back sarcastically, 'Is that so? Thank you!' His tone held not even a hint of gratitude.

'Tell me, how did that girl come looking for you?'

'She didn't come looking for me. She just happened to come to the house.'

'Did she say anything about having committed the murder?'

Having hidden the murderess, why not also hide the confession?

'No, she didn't say anything.'

'Why was she hiding?'

'She didn't tell me why.'

'Did she say anything at all? What was it?'

'All she went on saying was "Ayya, ayya, please save me!"'

'And what did you do?'

'I tried to talk to her in a reasonable way. She was like one possessed, all tightly strung up. I decided to keep talking to her in an unthreatening way till one of you arrived.'

'Where did she come from?'

'What her brother said was true. She had been hiding in that room. As we were talking the boy arrived and called "Akka!" And then he ran away to tell everyone in the village. She got rattled. "I'll run away, I'll run away," she started raving. I tried to stop her. I actually grabbed her, but she became violent and scratched me. Then she ran away.'

They searched upstairs in the hall; they searched the length and breadth of the garden and the woods nearby. They drew a blank. By now, Kalyanaraman's initial feeling of joy and relief had begun to ebb away. *Where could she be? What could possibly have happened to her in that room? I must investigate the room after these people leave.*

'If she comes back here …' began the inspector.

'I doubt she will come back,' Kalyanaraman assured him.

'Where can she go?' remarked Marudamuthu, still optimistic. 'She will be in our clutches before dawn. Finally she will have to go to her father. All we have to do is wait at her father's house … the chicken will itself fly into the trap.'

Exhausted by their exertions, the search party left for the village. The haloes of light from lanterns and torches dimmed to pinpoints and died away. An anaemic crescent moon hung over the treetops. Kalyanaraman was determined to overcome irrational fears. He bolted his room door from the inside and also shut the window that offered a view of the closed door to Snehalatha's room. Whatever doors and windows he tried to shut in the house, he couldn't shut those in his mind. He could picture Snehalatha's room, hear her laughter. He recalled little snippets of their conversation. 'You want to know when I will leave? I'll go, I'll go. Maybe a few days more …' 'I can clap my hands loudly, Ayyare!'

Besieged by memories of Snehalatha, Kalyanaraman absentmindedly clicked the tape recorder on.

'*On this jasmine-strewn mattress*
I've lain hardly a month…'

A sudden sound from somewhere … real or imagined? He was startled. 'Velli?' he called. Silence. He got up slowly, picked up the flashlight and went into the secret room. How could she have disappeared from here? 'Velli? Velli!'

That cupboard was the one behind which she had hidden earlier. She wasn't there. He swung the torch beam around. His eyes picked up something … he shone the light on it again. A faint footstep in the dust near the cupboard. Step here, and then somehow jump onto the top of the cupboard … no, there wasn't enough space to hide on the cupboard. He spotted a ventilator high in the wall. It was unbolted on the inside. It was faintly visible in the spillover of light from his room. A small opening, but a person could pass through with some difficulty.

Kalyanaraman could now visualize what must have happened. *Velli is hiding behind the cupboard. She hears the loud arguments and angry voices. She fears that the police will search the room again. She looks around desperately and spots the faint outline of the ventilator …*

But where can she have gone? The house and garden have been thoroughly searched. Where did her superhuman energy come from … the strength to climb up to a ventilator and wriggle through … for that matter, the strength to pick up a large stone and bring it down with great force on …

Anyway, she had got away. She should stay clear of her father's house. If she goes there, she's sure to be nabbed. They'll be waiting for her there. But then, where can she possibly be safe? The whole village is on the lookout for her. How long can she stay hidden? How far can she travel? And that too, alone and without help? The ventilator had shown her a providential way out for the time being. But for how many days? Or hours?

Kalyanaraman was afraid to go to sleep. He was afraid to turn off the light in the room. He now wished he had gone to the village with those men. 'Maybe I could have spent the night in Thangarasu's house, or even Marudamuthu's. How foolish of me to stay here tonight of all nights. It's best to get up and go to the village, even this late. But no, I can't go out in the night alone. I can't leave this room. Snehalatha is out there somewhere …'

The quavering voice of Peria Thatha, the old man who had come and offered to sing for him as he was leaving the villu paatu, played in Kalyanaraman's head.

'I believed the ship would come,
I waited on the shore.
The ship sank in the sea,
I now avoid the shore.
I had faith the boat would come,
I waited at the riverbank.
The boat drowned in the current,
I stay away from the river.'

And now the boat was approaching, backlit by the ghostly light of the moon. A black boat, with a single red light in front, bobbing and dancing on invisible waves. A jet-black boat … as black as death …

'I seek your blessings, Ayyare!'

And now Snehalatha is sitting somewhere out there with her back turned to him. Velli sneaks up on her, inch by inch, like Pazhayanur Neeli from the villu paatu. She has a large stone in her hand. She raises her hand high over Snehalatha's head. She is going to smash it down on her! No! No! Don't! Stop!

The arms grow numb, then the legs. The eyes stare blankly …

Sull … sull … salak … sull …

What's that sound? My God, this sound is real. It's not my mind playing tricks on me. Some woman is coming towards me. Yes, definitely a woman, and she is walking very slowly. Where did she come from? From the secret room? No, no. From Snehalatha's room? That cannot be. From outside … that's it. But why is she coming for me?

'To right three hundred wrongs
To seek revenge …'

'Ayyo! Who? What ...?' The fleeting thought went through his mind that he should get hold of a weapon. But he couldn't move. He could not even sit. He stood frozen to the spot, staring in a kind of perverse fascination at the approaching form.

She came into view. Loaded with jewellery. She was ... she was ... Ratnavathy! From the painting! The same Ratnavathy!

18

FOR A MOMENT OR two his tired eyes and fogged brain had told him this was Ratnavathy herself, come back to life and approaching him in the dark of night. She was soaked to the skin and beads of water trickled from her forehead. She was adorned with heavy jewellery, just like in her portrait … a large *chutti* hiding the parting of her hair, a ruby-studded pendant around her neck, an ornate circlet clinging to her upper arm …

As she came closer, the trance was broken.

'Velli! What's all this!' he exclaimed in astonishment.

'Jewels! I found them. They're mine. There are more, many more … sun and moon ornaments, chokers, nose rings, finger rings, ear studs, chains … so many things.'

'Ey, stop it!'

Velli was like a woman possessed. She feverishly stroked and handled the jewellery, took them off and put them on again. 'Mine, mine!' she said again and again. 'I found them.'

'Where did you go? Where were you hiding?'

'Inside the well in the garden. My God, so many jewels! Nose rings, ear studs …'

'Stop. Where did you find the jewels?'

'Inside the well, where I was hiding. They are in a box in a hole in the wall. See, the well is wide and there are bricks sticking out on the inside wall for people to climb down. When I was hiding in the room behind the cupboard, I was sure they would discover me and finish me off. So I climbed up to the ventilator and crawled out. Then I hid upstairs for a while and then crept out into the garden in the darkness and made my way to the well.

'They came with lanterns searching for me all over the garden. I climbed into the well, held my breath and hid under the water. When they went away I started climbing out. I was tired and out of breath, so I sat on a kind of narrow ledge halfway up the wall. Something brushed against my arm. It was a tin box, hidden inside a niche near the ledge. I drew it out and opened it … My goodness! What a shock I got! The light was very dim, yet the things inside glittered! So much jewellery … I found it!'

Kalyanaraman took a closer look at the ornaments Velli was wearing. He immediately recognized some of them as being the same ones worn by Ratnavathy in the portrait. So Velli had found Ratnavathy's hidden treasure. But how had the box of jewels ended up in the well?

'All the jewels belong to me. I found them. You will give them to me, won't you?'

'Yes, wear rich clothes, load yourself with jewellery and hang yourself! What a silly creature you are! Is jewellery the most important thing right now?' He handed her a towel. 'Here, dry yourself off first.'

The first order of business was to cover up her chest. Her breasts were clearly visible through her wet clothes … very distracting …

Recollections of past events flashed through Kalyanaraman's mind. 'Marudamuthu with the thick rope. Why the rope? I must ask him. Did Snehalatha use him to track down the treasure?'

Velli was still totally absorbed in admiring her newfound riches.

'Ey, Velli! Your life is in danger, and you are going crazy over jewellery! The whole village is on the job of hunting you down and you are strutting around wearing all this stuff.'

'I'll give a piece to each of them and they will leave me alone.'

'Don't be an idiot!'

As reality struck her, Velli's expression changed. She looked abashed. 'See, it's true I am an idiot. Jewels are not important now. Did you hear the way that man talked about me?'

'Which man?'

'Marudamuthu, who else? He talked as if he didn't care for me at all. Maybe he is still thinking of that woman …'

'He is furious that you killed her. If he sets eyes on you, he will likely murder you.'

'True, saar. It will take some more days for him to see reason and come around.'

'Long before that you would have been caught and locked away. Look, Velli, why did you do it? Is it fair to take a person's life over a small matter?'

'I didn't plan to kill her, saar. In the heat of the moment I picked up a stone and … Amman gave me the strength …'

'Ayyo, Ayyo! Can we forget Amman for a while? Where is the stone you used?'

'It must be lying around the place somewhere.'

'A granite stone?'

'Yes.'

'And you threw it at her head?'

'No, saar, it would have missed her head.'

'Did she scream "Ayyo"? Did she groan in pain?'

'No, she wouldn't have felt pain.'

'What do you mean? How could she not feel pain when a big stone lands on her?'

'But it was such a small stone.'

'What? A small stone? How small?'

Velli held out a hand with the thumb and forefinger about an inch apart.

'About that big.'

'What … what are you saying, Velli?'

'I mean, how can such a small stone cause any pain?'

'Velli, are you saying that one small pebble is all that you threw at Snehalatha?'

'Yes, yes.'

'And yet she died?'

'Yes. Because of the spell cast by the pujari. He told me it was powerful.'

'My God! What a fool you are. Can a person die if a pebble the size of a tamarind seed is flung at her? Don't you know even that much?'

'I'm not saying the stone itself killed her. But it contained a magic spell, you see? I sacrificed a chicken, then there was the doll and the vibhuti … all these things together made her spit blood and die. You won't understand, saar. It is all Amman's strength …'

Kalyanaraman slapped himself on the forehead in frustration. Imagine such ignorant souls going around in society! 'You foolish, foolish girl! And just for this you became terrified and hid here and there for two days!'

With a wry smile he asked, 'Velli, did you really believe you caused Snehalatha's death? Or is this some elaborate drama? I understand people can be superstitious, but that doesn't mean they take leave of their common sense! Oh bloody hell!'

'What are you saying, saar?'

'Look, someone else murdered Snehalatha. It wasn't you and it wasn't your Amman.'

'No, no, saar, I did it. I threw a stone …'

'Don't be a stubborn idiot, Velli. Listen to me. You … have … not … killed … anyone. Understand? You don't have to run away, you don't have to hide. That tiny stone you threw could never have killed her.' The thought of it made him laugh.

'But the pujari said …'

'That pujari fellow is a fraud. You believed him and came here that night with that silly doll and some vibhuti that he had given you. Then you scolded Snehalatha, threw a tiny stone at her, left the doll and vibhuti near her and went away. That's what happened, right?'

'Yes, that's what I did.'

'When you shouted at her and abused her, did she reply?'

'Mm ... hmm, no.'

'Not even a single word?'

'No, nothing.'

'Where was she?'

'She was sort of crouching in the doorway. It was dark ...'

'Ah, now it's clear what happened. You silly creature, listen to me carefully. *When you came here that night Snehalatha was already dead!* Not knowing that, you scolded her, threw a small stone at her and went away. The next day you heard she had been killed overnight. So you panicked and hid away. Isn't that so?' Kalyanaraman smiled as he spoke.

'Yes, yes. But why are you laughing, saar?'

'What can I do except laugh at your stupidity!'

'Yes, I'm stupid. I can't read or write. I'm ignorant. Do you really mean I didn't kill her?'

'You definitely did not kill her. You needn't be afraid of the police or anyone else. And you don't have to hide any longer.'

Even as he spoke he realized that the revelation of Velli's innocence had raised another urgent question. 'Who is the real murderer? Could it be Marudamuthu?'

Velli began taking off the jewellery. 'I don't want these any longer, ayya.'

'Wait ... wait.'

Jewels! thought Kalyanaraman. *They are the motive for Snehalatha's murder. She must have deliberately come under a false identity to steal the treasure.*

'Velli, will you show me the hiding place of the jewel box?'

'Yes, but if I go out in the open, they will see me and ...'

'No one will harm you. Come with me. We must get to that treasure before the rest of them arrive.'

When the two of them stepped outside, the whole orb of the sun was above the eastern horizon. The birds were trying out their voices in preparation for the new day. The sky was cloudless; the leaves on the trees hung unmoving.

Kalyanaraman noticed a dried bloodstain just outside the door to Snehalatha's room. That must have been the spot where she was killed. He himself had arrived just when the killer was dragging the body to the well. He remembered hearing footsteps running away. Gradually, the curtain of confusion that had obscured the happenings of that fateful night was being lifted. The sequence of events was now clearer in his mind.

Snehalatha leaves while the villu paatu is going on, and Marudamuthu follows soon afterwards. The two of them go into Snehalatha's room. Velli comes there and discovers them together in the room. After a brief exchange of heated words with Marudamuthu, she returns home, downhearted. Apparently Snehalatha has allowed Marudamuthu some degree of intimacy. Was it as a reward for his help with her plan to steal the treasure? What kind of help? Did that rope have something to do with it?

And what happened next? Did Marudamuthu go away leaving Snehalatha alive and alone? In which case, who came there later …?

Kalyanaraman and Velli arrived at the garden well. It was indeed a wide one, as Velli had described it. On the inner wall, protruding bricks provided a spiral path downwards to the water's surface. The water was greenish; as they peered over the parapet, they could see their faces reflected in it.

'Look there near the tenth step,' said Velli pointing down into the well. 'Do you see that hole in the side? That's where the box is.'

Velli descended rapidly to the ledge she had indicated. 'Come along and look!' she called out. Kalyanaraman made a far more cautious and gingerly descent.

'Velli, do you know how to swim?'

'Yes, ayya. What about you?'

'I have swum in the college swimming pool in Madras, but I have never entered a well …'

'Don't worry, the water is no deeper than the height of one and a half men.'

'Isn't that deep enough!' A bit of plaster came loose from the wall and splashed into the water. A frog made a high dive and another splash. Kalyanaraman arrived safely at the ledge. He drew the box out of the crevice. The brass latch had turned green, and the whole box showed signs of having been immersed in water for a long time. He opened it …

Inside lay what appeared to be Ratnavathy's entire collection of jewellery. Having been piled together hastily and immersed in water, their brightness had indeed dimmed somewhat. Even so, their splendour was breathtaking. Gold ornaments studded with diamonds, sapphires, emeralds and rubies. For just a moment Kalyanaraman had a fleeting desire to take the whole lot and disappear. 'No, no,' he cautioned himself, 'remember these are hereditary jewels with a history. They have caused a murder.'

'Velli, take off all those jewels that you are wearing and put them back in the box.'

She did so obediently. He climbed out and reached down to help her. 'Come, hold my hand.' He deliberately brushed his fingers against her breast.

Here is a girl who is now totally under my spell. She is ready to do whatever I ask of her. A girl like that, a box of jewels like that, how easy it would be to take both treasures and slip away under the cover of nightfall.

His other inner voice took over. *Mm … hmm. No, no. You should not leave the village till this murder mystery is solved. You have to know who killed Snehalatha.*

The box was back where it had been with its contents intact, and the two of them had climbed out of the well. Kalyanaraman looked around. A tree … a champaka tree … there, quite close to the well. And a dead champaka flower pressed into the pages of Ratnavathy's diary. He remembered Snehalatha opening the diary to that page, showing him the flower, and asking him, 'Do you know what kind of flower this is?'

His thoughts swirled and settled into a pattern.

Ratnavathy had written, 'I've kept a champaka flower as a sign.' A sign of what? Perhaps a clue to the location of the treasure? She had said in her diary, 'I've come to a decision, I won't give my jewels to anyone. No one should have them. I've found a way to make sure of that. I will put all of them …'

Where? Where did you put them, Ratnavathy? Did you put them all in a box and throw them into the well? And did you leave a pressed champaka flower as a sign that the jewels were near a champaka tree?

Snehalatha must have made the connection … champaka flower, champaka tree, the well, jewellery. That's why she needed Marudamuthu's help, and that thick rope. They had probably pulled the box out from under the water the previous night itself and hidden it in that crevice to retrieve later. But then maybe they had a fight and Marudamuthu killed Snehalatha?

His train of thought was disturbed when Velli whispered urgently, 'Ayya, we have to go now.'

'Why, Velli?'

'Look over there! So many men. It looks like the whole village is coming here.'

Kalyanaraman turned and looked. About thirty men, armed with bamboo poles, were advancing menacingly towards the well. Leading the group was Marudamuthu, brandishing a sharp sickle. Alongside strode the inspector, Periasamy, Ayyadurai, Thangarasu … all of them.

'Ayya, I'll go and hide,' whispered Velli.

'No, Velli, there is no longer any need for you to hide. I will manage the situation.'

19

MARUDAMUTHU WAS AT THE head of the approaching group of men. Velli hurried towards him.

'Oh, there you are! Now you are trapped. Come here, di.'

Velli stopped dead in her tracks. She was taken aback by his hostility.

'Inspector, saar, this is the missing girl who has been playing hide-and-seek with us over the last couple of days. Nab her before she gets away again,' urged Marudamuthu. 'Ey, Moodevi, go and fall at Inspector Ayya's feet, di.'

He glared at Kalyanaraman. 'Ayya, you should not have told us so many lies. We blindly believed you …'

The inspector stepped forward. 'Hold on, Marudamuthu, let me handle this. Kalyanaraman, don't you know it's against the law to harbour a wanted criminal? Ey, pilla, come over here.' The latter order was addressed to Velli.

Velli looked at Kalyanaraman pleadingly, confusion and uncertainty in her eyes.

Insults flew thick and fast at Velli.

'Che! Is this a woman? No, She is Neeli, Bhadrakali!'

'Look how she is standing there brazenly after committing murder!'

Kalyanaraman tried to save her from the verbal barbs. 'Velli, go and stay inside the house. Inspector, she is an ignorant girl. She blindly believed what the pujari told her. She believed she was responsible for Snehalatha's death. But she was not. She is innocent. She followed that pujari fellow's advice and cast some foolish spells and flung a small stone at Snehalatha.

That was all. But when she heard that Snehalatha had died, she panicked and went into hiding. If you talk to her, it will all become clear.'

'No, no, this man is her accomplice, saar!' said Marudamuthu.

Velli cut in angrily. 'What rubbish! Just wait and see what I do to you! How dare you drag this ayya into this? It is for your sake that I went through all this torture. I had to walk for miles and hide here and there ... don't be such an ungrateful wretch.'

Marudamuthu was boiling with rage. 'Oh, shut up! I'll smack you! You've both carried out this murder together, and now you are spinning a web of lies!'

Kalyanaraman interceded. 'Inspector, Marudamuthu is the one who needs to be interrogated. Ask him about that thick rope he brought here secretly one night. I'll prove who was abetting murder. What do you say, Marudamuthu? Remember the rope you brought secretly after dark?'

'You evil fellow! Murderer! How dare you talk like that!' Marudamuthu swung his arm and hit Kalyanaraman in the face with the back of his hand.

Kalyanaraman was stunned by this unexpected show of violence. Tears sprang to his eyes. 'What ... Inspector! You are just standing there and watching him hit me.'

'Dei, stop hitting him,' ordered the inspector, not very convincingly. 'You're not going to achieve anything that way.' He touched Velli's arm. She shook him off. 'Come inside, pilla. I have to question you. Periasamy. Stay here. Make sure there is no fighting. No blows. Only words may be used.'

He half-pushed and half-dragged a reluctant Velli towards the house. Kalyanaraman felt sick to his stomach. He tried to message her telepathically. *'Velli, please don't blurt out anything that may make him suspicious of you. Remember you are not responsible for Snehalatha's death. You have committed no crime.'*

'Give this fellow a beating!' called out someone. A slim fellow from the group, emboldened by the support of his friends, came forward and landed a blow on Kalyanaraman. The latter grabbed his assailant's arm and twisted it sharply. 'Ayyo!' shouted the thin fellow in pain.

Marudamuthu had been waiting for just such a thing to happen. 'Oh, so you are attacking us now, eh? Periasamy, you are the witness. We are beating this Brahmin chap only in self-defence. He attacked us.'

Periasamy seemed to be complicit in the plot to give Kalyanaraman a thrashing. He now said something totally unjust to Kalyanaraman. 'Ayya, in this kind of situation, when there is strong suspicion against you in a serious crime, why did you hurt that young man? Now how can I protect you from the fury of these people?'

Kalyanaraman broke into a cold sweat. There were eight sturdy men ranged against him. They came closer; they surrounded him. 'Don't! Don't hit me!'

The blows rained down from all directions. Hip, chest, back, knees, what part of him could he protect from this mob? If he fell to the ground, they could even trample him to death. If he resisted violently, it would stoke even greater violence. They were drunk with anger. 'Your only hope is to reach the zamin house,' he told himself. 'If you run in the opposite direction, across the fields, they will catch up with you and finish you off. Run!'

He stumbled and almost fell, but struggled upright. There was blood on his shirt, a hard fist landed on his jaw. He lowered his head and, with some newfound burst of energy, pushed aside two of his assailants and started running towards the house.

'Inspector! Inspector! Save me!' he shouted as he ran at a speed born of desperation. The door to his room was shut, and the inspector was on the verandah smoking a cigarette. Making an instant decision, he veered towards Snehalatha's room, ran in, and bolted the door.

The pursuers landed up at the entrance to the building. One of them called out to Kalyanaraman, 'Come out, you coward! We will tear you limb from limb!'

Kalyanaraman continued to appeal to the inspector's sense of duty. 'Inspector, it is your duty to protect me. Standing by and watching while they beat me up is not acceptable behaviour.'

'Who hit you?' challenged Periasamy. 'No one hit you.'

But someone from the group called out, 'Let that Brahmin fellow out. We will finish him off right here.'

'Che! Go away, da,' ordered the inspector. 'Don't create a scene. I'll take care of matters. Marudamuthu, go and tell Ayyadurai to bring the report forms. That girl is weeping nonstop. I think she's scared because she had to hide away for two days.'

'Why should she be afraid unless she is guilty of the murder?'

'Inspector,' urged Kalyanaraman, 'don't let Marudamuthu get away. Ask him what he and Snehalatha drew out of the well. Ask him the value of what they lifted out. I know exactly why Snehalatha came here and what her plan was. Give me a chance to clear up a few things, and I will tell you the whole story.'

The inspector was caught in two minds. 'Marudamuthu, what is this about?'

'He is bluffing, saar. I will tell you all the details if you will come with me.'

'No, no, don't believe him. He's a liar,' insisted Kalyanaraman. 'He has abetted the crime.'

Marudamuthu picked up a pebble, flung it at the window of Snehalatha's room in which Kalyanaraman had locked himself, and stuck out his tongue in defiance. 'Wait and see how I deal with you!' he shouted. 'Come, saar,' he invited the inspector, 'let us move away over there.'

Kalyanaraman watched through the window as Marudamuthu and the inspector made their leisurely way down the verandah steps into the garden and strolled along talking in a friendly fashion. From the window opposite, Velli's desperate face pleaded silently for help. Outside, among the group, a particularly crude young fellow stripped off his dhoti and gyrated in his underwear, taunting Kalyanaraman, 'Come out here and get a thrashing!'

'These people are all against me,' thought Kalyanaraman. 'They are not going to believe me … not even the inspector will listen.'

A little way down the garden, the inspector and Marudamuthu had stopped walking and were chatting earnestly, heads close together. Meanwhile, Periatha was approaching the house, along with Velli's father.

'Velli, my dear child, what a terrible thing you've done!' wailed the father.

Periatha was not to be outdone. '*Emmadi, emmadi! Seemayile cheerazhinji* … Look how they have caged my darling! Who will pass judgement? Will they lock her in a prison cell?'

Velli, sobbing as she spoke, said, 'It wasn't me, Periatha. Appa, I didn't kill her. Someone else has murdered her to steal jewellery.'

'The two of you have been locked in separate rooms,' observed Periatha.

'Yes, atha.'

'When are they going to bring the cart?' As she was talking, Periatha went up close and looked through the window of the room in which Kalyanaraman had locked himself. She saw his bruises.

'Oh, you are such a noble ayya! A prince! Che, they have dared to beat you!' She paused to open her string bag, take out a wad of betel leaves and fold them into her mouth. Her gaze darted all around the room. 'Don't worry, ayya. Nothing will happen to you. I know you both, and I know you could not have done such a deed. You want any witnesses to come forward to help you? Give me some money and I will arrange for that.'

'No, no, I don't want anything like that, Periatha.'

'Have they cremated that woman's body?'

'I don't know.'

'What? What did you say?'

'I said I ... don't ... know! Why don't you go away now and come later.'

'That's a good idea,' agreed Periatha, moving away.

Kalyanaraman looked carefully around him. All Snehalatha's belongings seemed to be intact and undisturbed. Clothing of various kinds … jeans, dresses … hung from hangers on a clothesline that had been strung across the room. He opened the cupboard. Snehalatha's makeup kit and toiletry articles filled virtually the entire space. Lipsticks, face powders, creams, several colours of pottus, a small key, little bottles of green and red liquids that Kalyanaraman could not identify ... wait! A small key!

Snehalatha's suitcase was under the bed. Kalyanaraman was reminded of how Snehalatha had taken Ratnavathy's diary from his hand and locked it in her suitcase.

He peeped out cautiously into the garden. People were standing around and chatting idly in small groups. Periasamy was smoking a beedi. Periatha and Velli's father were talking to Velli through the window. 'Don't worry, ma. We can hire a big lawyer in the town,' her father was assuring her.

No one was paying any attention to Kalyanaraman.

He pulled the suitcase from under the bed and opened it. Lots of papers; a couple of saris; a photo album (surprise!); a jumble of clothes; a thick file; and under the whole heap of things … Ratnavathy's diary!

Hurriedly, he turned the pages. The page marked with the pressed champaka flower ('I have left a sign'); 'family jewels, belonging to my grandmother's grandmother, all melted, pawned' (already read); 'I have gathered the remaining jewels together and put them ...' (yes, that was where he had been interrupted). He read on feverishly.

> I have put them in a box which I have stored in a safe place. I have left a sign about the hiding place of the box. This is the clue [champaka flower]. Let my jewels stay there. Let some clever people find them sometime. My jewels should not go to this man [her husband]. Even if he scolds me, threatens me, beats me, tortures me ... or kills me ... I shall stand firm on this decision. I don't think I have long to live. This man is killing me inch by inch. Visalakshi, Muthamma, I pray to you, please take me away. Why should I continue to exist in this loveless state?
>
> If there are any good, honest citizens in this land ... ayya, if you are such a person and find my jewellery, I, Ratnavathy, plead with folded hands that you should take the whole lot and distribute it as charity among the poor in my name ... in dead Ratnavathy's name.
>
> These jewels should never come into the hands of anyone in this family. Never, never, never! This book is the only place where I have written about this. So I am hiding it where it will not be easily discovered. If sometime in the future, some stranger, totally unconnected to this family, comes and finds and reads this ... and if he can shed a tear for the memory of a woman who never received a day's affection from her husband and who died in despair and grief, I shall be grateful enough.

Ratnavathy ... Ratna ... rattham. A dried bloodstain on the page.

The following pages were blank. As he riffled through them, a letter fell out of the book.

Chennai-16

16-6-78

Dear Snake,

We have now come to the second part of our plan. Come at once. I have searched all around for a month with no success. I hear that a researcher of folk music from the city is due to come to the village and he will be staying at the zamin house. That will cause complications for us. Get here fast.

Remember everything I told you. Names, names, names. And you are the chinna zamindar's daughter.

And Snake, we are partners in this, so no double-crossing! The treasure is priceless.

Good Luck!

Sami

'My God!' exclaimed Kalyanaraman inwardly. The murky scene was clearing. It was like holding up a banknote to the light and watching the outline of the lion's-head watermark appear. He thought for a moment and then called out, 'Inspector!' The inspector seemed to have left. Only Periasamy was visible at a distance. Velli and her father were still talking together.

The matter was now very urgent. Some things had to be done immediately. 'I need to get to Thirunilam town. But how? And before that I have to get down into that well once more ...'

Snehalatha's room had a side door leading into the garden away from the line of sight of those at the front of the house. As he opened the door and stepped out onto the side verandah, the well was visible at the far end.

He walked carefully and quietly. No one noticed his departure. He came to the champaka tree, Snehalatha's secret clue. He descended into the well.

The collector's office in Thirunilam was in an old building dating back to the days of the sultans. Green mat screens hung over the windows to protect against the midday heat, and attendants were wetting the khus-khus coverings for extra coolness.

Inside, people were waiting to meet the collector. When Kalyanaraman walked into the collector's waiting room after a long walk through fields in the heat, a khadi-clad assistant, somewhat wary of the appearance of this dishevelled visitor, said, 'Collector Ayya isn't here. You can't meet him.'

'When will he come?'

'I don't know.'

'Who will know.'

'His PA.'

'Can I meet him?'

'Pah! What a nuisance. Go away and come ... Oh, good morning, sir!'

This last greeting was to the collector who had unexpectedly appeared.

The collector looked Kalyanaraman up and down, taking in his scratched arms and ripped clothes.

'Who are you, ayya?'

'Sir, I met you at Mempatti. My name is Kalyanaraman.'

'Ah, yes! Kalyanaraman. Folk music! Those children ... you had taught them to sing in chorus.'

'Yes, sir.'

'How is Snehalatha?'

'She is dead.'

'Oh, my God! How?'

'That's why I've come here to meet you.'

'Come into my office.'

The collector, one hand supporting his chin, sat and listened to the whole story.

'Very interesting!' he remarked.

'Look at this piece of jewellery,' said Kalyanaraman, holding out an item he had retrieved from the box in the well. 'There are a hundred pieces of different kinds.'

The collector took the ornament and inspected it closely, turning it over in his hands. Kalyanaraman elaborated further.

'The letter makes it clear that the two of them were in the plot together. The man came ahead and searched but found nothing, so he asked Snehalatha to come. She pretended to be the old zamindar's granddaughter. She managed to come across the diary and worked out where the jewels were hidden. She took Marudamuthu's help, and the two of them hauled the box out from under the water. Meanwhile, the second schemer, the one who wrote the letter, somehow came to know about the discovery of the treasure. He probably came late at night and demanded his share. She may have refused, and so he killed her.'

'But who is this second schemer?'

'He will be easy to find, sir. I thought at first that Snehalatha and Marudamuthu must have hidden the box temporarily in that crevice in the well. But, if I am right, and this is how everything happened, that second schemer is the one who would have hidden it there. He would have planned to wait for the scent to grow cold. He will come to the well one of these nights. We just have to wait in hiding and nab him.'

'Oh, yes!' The collector reached for his telephone. 'Connect me to the police superintendent.'

20

AS ARRANGED BY THE collector, a superintendent of police accompanied Kalyanaraman to the village. They arrived at four in the evening and went directly to the zamindar's house. There was no one around. The door to Kalyanaraman's room was locked from the outside. When they looked through the window, they saw Velli stretched out on the floor. She could have tried to get away, but where could she go?

The superintendent of police who had accompanied Kalyanaraman was a young man, evidently a recent recruit to the post. He had hardly spoken to Kalyanaraman. On their drive to the village in a jeep, he had remained reserved and distant.

'That is the young woman Velli that I told you about,' said Kalyanaraman.

From the back of the house a voice called out, 'Who's there?' Periasamy and Periatha came into view around the corner of the building. Periatha, that eternal raider of treasures from trees, had a sari-fold full of various fruits, many unfamiliar to Kalyanaraman. Periasamy's jaws were busy munching something. When he saw the superintendent, he paled visibly and rushed forward to greet him with folded hands. 'Ayya!'

'Who are you?'

'A constable, saar.'

'Where's your uniform?'

'I've given it for starching.' Then, turning to Periatha, 'Ey, you old hag, come and do a namaskaram to this important ayya.'

'My namaskarams, ayya. Oh, what a fine young man you are! You look like a prince!'

'First open this door. Who locked her in here?'

'The inspector, saar,' said Periasamy, rushing to unlock the door.

'Go and fetch the inspector,' ordered the superintendent as he opened the door and stepped in.

As usual, Periatha wanted a piece of the attention. She squeezed into the room behind the superintendent. 'Velli, my dear, dear angel. Get up, my beautiful ruby. See who has come. He is going to set you free, this prince. Oh you beautiful coconut sapling, you've been planted in slush …'

'Sh! Old woman, keep quiet!' ordered the superintendent sternly. Then, addressing the prisoner, 'So you are Velli? Get up and come out of the room, ma.'

Velli clutched her dirty, stained clothes close and inched out hesitantly, panic in her eyes. Mud and dirt covered her back, and her blouse was torn. An angry red scratch ran across her cheek. Bare arms, bangles broken and gone; bare forehead, the pottu wiped away long since. She was a picture of total exhaustion.

'Velli, don't be afraid. You are innocent, so you will be set free. Have you eaten anything?'

'No,' she murmured, and began to weep. She looked at them, sniffled, wiped her nose on her dirty sari, and sobbed again.

'How did they ever suspect her and lock her up? Che! One look at her eyes tells you she is innocent!' remarked the superintendent.

'Ayya, when he comes, tell him that.'

'When who comes?'

'Marudamuthu. The one who has ditched this girl.'

'What do you want me to tell him?'

Velli asked Kalyanaraman eagerly, 'Did ayya hear the whole story?'

'Yes, this ayya is a very senior police officer.'

'Oh! Such an important person! Ayya, please tell that man when he comes. Please give him good advice. Tell him that he has behaved very badly. He fell under that woman's spell and hurt me. He has made me so miserable. Be harsh! Make him regret what he has done to me.'

'All right, all right. But you should go home now and eat something,' replied the superintendent.

'No, no. If they see me in the village they will attack me and throw stones at me. Please let me stay here.'

'Where is your father, Velli?' asked Kalyanaraman.

'He has gone to the town to fetch a lawyer.'

'*Adiammadi!*' exclaimed Periatha. 'How stubbornly loyal you are! You are prepared to make enemies of everyone else just to stick by this ass of a fellow just because of some kind of understanding that you would marry him. He has been false to you. So why don't you just tell him, this is the end of any relationship between the two of you?'

'Yes, tell her, Periatha,' urged Kalyanaraman. 'Put some good sense into her head.'

While Periatha and Velli sat and talked on the verandah, Kalyanaraman led the superintendent to the well. They both peered into it. Their reflected images gazed back at them.

'Look near the tenth step down from the top,' Kalyanaraman told him. 'You will see a hole in the side of the wall. There is a box in that hole, full of precious jewels. I'd guess their value runs to several lakhs.'

Bending over to look for the hole that Kalyanaraman was pointing out, the superintendent remarked, 'Is that so!' He picked up a pebble and tossed it into the well. Their two reflected images rippled and broke up.

'Take an inventory of the contents and give a statement to the collector,' said the superintendent. 'The jewels can be deposited in the Thirunilam treasury.'

'We can do that only tomorrow, sir. We should wait to see if the culprit turns up here tonight to retrieve the treasure.'

'Right,' agreed the police officer.

The two of them went back to the house. As they approached the front of the building, the inspector was just arriving, along with Periasamy. The inspector offered a crisp salute to his superior officer. Periasamy was now in his uniform.

'You're S.S. Kandiah, right?' asked the superintendent.

'Yes, sir,' responded the inspector. 'I was …'

'I remember. You were at Vilathikulam earlier. Why have you detained this young woman?'

'It was a missing person case, sir. Plus she was a suspect in the murder. So we kept her confined as a precaution. In such matters even village officials can take action.'

'After a police inspector has taken over a case, no village official has even an ounce of power. Did you mishandle the woman?'

'No, sir.'

'You are lying. When it comes to women suspects, only women police should deal with them. Don't you know that? I heard about everything that happened. The case has taken a new turn. Where's the body? Is the postmortem over?'

'Yes, sir. The body is in the town hospital.'

'What arrangements have you made for the burial? Do you just want to keep the body rolled in a mat for days waiting to be buried? Talk to the wealthy village elder, Ayyadurai. All the arrangements have to be made. You, constable, what's your name?'

'Periasamy, saar.'

'Periasamy, go and stand over there at the end of the garden.'

When Periasamy had moved out of earshot, the superintendent gave the inspector a series of instructions. 'Bring this young woman Velli and that old Periatha to the town. Let them stay there together for a day or two. Meanwhile, spread a rumour in the village that Velli has been arrested for murder and taken away by the police. Also, let the word spread that the case has been wrapped up, and so the police have locked up the zamindar's house and gone away. Do you understand?'

'Yes, sir!'

'Someone in the village must have committed the murder. That woman came and set herself up here under false pretences. Obviously she came looking for the hidden treasure and managed to trace it. Then some kind of quarrel must have taken place between her and her accomplice. The jewels are hidden inside a well in the garden of this house. I expect the murderer will return at night to pick up the treasure. We will all leave here now and give the impression that we have finished our work here. But we will come back at night and stay hidden, waiting for whoever comes to the well. We will nab him there.'

'Periasamy and I will come with you . . .' offered the inspector.

'No, Periasamy need not come. I'm not completely sure he isn't involved in some way. You and I alone will come back and wait.'

The superintendent set the wheels of the plan in motion. 'Periasamy, come here! Take these two women to that jeep parked over there. We are going to arrest Velli now.'

It was one o'clock in the morning. The two police officers were hiding somewhere near the well. Kalyanaraman was also in hiding, but in a different place, near the peepul tree. The moon was still making up its mind about whether to venture out into the sky. Black shadows in various shapes lay everywhere, like large Rorschach inkblots. An owl screeched like a sharp nail drawn across a slate. A couple of the birds flapped their heavy wings and landed confidently on the parapet of the well. They also waited.

Kalyanaraman's senses were on high alert. Tonight the identity of the murderer would be revealed, and the mystery would be solved. Who would approach the well under cover of darkness? The one who had signed his letter to Snehalatha as 'Sami' would soon appear at the well. Would it be the pujari? Or Periasamy? Or even Thangarasu? Oh, che, none of those could possibly be the one. Anyway, whoever came during the night would surely be the one who had committed the murder.

This man and Snehalatha had plotted together to steal the jewels. The man had come first and searched high and low for a month, but he had drawn a blank. Then he wrote a letter summoning his friend Snehalatha, or 'Snake' as he addressed her, and signed it as 'Sami'. After she had found the treasure, he must have decided to eliminate his partner in crime …

Someone was approaching with slow, deliberate, firm steps. With each footfall, dry leaves crumbled underfoot, rustling in the stillness of the night … *sarak* ... *sarak*. Whoever it was seemed unhurried and confident.

Kalyanaraman held his breath. It was important not to give the new arrival any hint that others were around. If he had the least suspicion, he would run away. Now Kalyanaraman could make out the approaching figure as a darker silhouette against the enveloping darkness. *Sarak*, *sarak* … spoke the dry leaves ... and then came the scratching sound of a matchstick being lit ... *kreech*. Kalyanaraman froze in the wide shadow of the peepul tree. Careful! Careful!

The dark form approached the well. *Wait, wait, Inspector! Superintendent sir, wait! Don't make a move yet!* urged Kalyanaraman's mind, trying to convey telepathic messages to the police officers.

The mysterious person struck another match and peered into the well. When the light died out, yet another match flared, and whoever it was climbed over the parapet and descended slowly into the well.

Now Kalyanaraman saw two other forms cautiously approaching the well. He recognized them as the police officers who had been in hiding. *Careful! Don't rush! Wait … wait …*

The seconds crept by. The moon had picked up enthusiasm and was beaming happily. A head appeared above the parapet. The two officers ducked out of sight. Soon thereafter, a commotion broke out.

'No, no, let me go. I don't know anything!' A man's voice, sounding terrified.

Thuk! A cane landing with force on a knee. 'Ayyo!' The man in agony. *Clang*! The sound of a metal box falling to the ground.

The policemen dragged the mystery man back to the house and into a room and turned on the light. Kalyanaraman followed them. The inspector pushed the man into a corner, grabbed a handful of his hair and raised his face to the light.

'Have you seen this fellow before?' he asked Kalyanaraman.

Kalyanaraman looked into the frightened face. Where had he seen it earlier …?

'I've seen him, but I can't remember where. Let me think for a moment. Was it at the village festival … no, it was earlier than that … that moustache and hair, kajal in the eyes … oh, yes! Ey, aren't you Bioscope Pazhaniandi?'

The more he looked at the man's face, the more sure Kalyanaraman was. He could now remember exactly how he had been dressed at the time. A felt hat, a flower behind his ear, an anklet, a badly fitting coat. With these extras missing at this moment, it had taken Kalyanaraman longer to place him.

'Sir, this fellow used to go around carrying a black box with a peephole through which he showed films to entertain people for a fee. Everyone in the village knows him well, particularly the children.'

'Ey, what's your name, da?'

'What he said … I'm Bioscope Pazhaniandi.'

'That's only your false identity. Who are you really?'

'I don't know anything.'

'If that's so, why did you come to the well in the middle of the night, climb down and bring out this box? What's in the box?'

'I don't know.'

'What did you do to Snehalatha?'

'I don't know anything.'

Thwack! A resounding slap landed on Bioscope Man's face. Kalyanaraman flinched at the sound.

'I don't know anything. Let me go, saar.'

'We can easily take your fingerprints and prove your guilt. In a bloodstain on Snehalatha's room wall we have a palm print of the murderer ... all five fingers.'

'I didn't do anything.'

'Mister Kalyanaraman, please leave the room,' said the superintendent.

'No, no. Ayya, please don't go. They will finish me off. Please stay here. Please!'

'We're not going to do anything to him. You can step out.'

Kalyanaraman confronted the cowering figure of Bioscope Man. 'Enda, when you were murdering that woman, what agony she would have suffered!'

'I didn't murder her! I didn't!'

'Don't waste your time talking to this fellow,' advised the superintendent. 'Go to the village and find a place to sleep. By morning we will have this fellow's confession.'

As Kalyanaraman moved away, he could hear the beginning of the interrogation.

'All right, Bioscope Pazhaniandi, where are you from?'

'Mekalapuram.'

'Which street in Mekalapuram?'

'Mettu Street.'

'There is no such street in Mekalapuram.'

Kalyanaraman began walking slowly away from the zamin house towards the village. Gradually, the occasional sounds of Bioscope Man's screams also faded out of earshot. As he went further away from that house, his feeling of dread dropped away and he walked like an automaton in a kind of semi-daze. There was already faint light on the eastern horizon. Dawn was not far away. The birds began trying out their voices. He came to the pond with its hazy reflection of the zamin house, the two wells at the edge of the village, the fierce figure of Kathaveeraiyan, the two horses, the silhouette of Ayyanar ... all the familiar landmarks of Mempatti. Many of the village folk were already up and about.

Kalyanaraman made his way to Thangarasu's house. He called from outside, 'Thangarasu, I need to sleep.'

'All right, but the sun is about to rise ...'

'Let it rise.'

He lay on a bed in a small room in Thangarasu's house, next to a pile of stored grain. Even as Thangarasu was switching on the ceiling fan and asking, 'Are you comfortable?' Kalyanaraman fell into a deep sleep.

'Kalyanaraman, wake up! He has confessed. He is the son of the old zamindar's mistress.'

21

THE BLADES OF THE ceiling fan circled languidly overhead as the collector summed up the case. Seated facing him were the superintendent of police, the inspector, Kalyanaraman and the village elder, Ayyadurai.

A clerk, wearing a faint *naamam* on his forehead, brought a file to the collector's table, leaned forward, and opened it just enough for the collector to view the contents.

The collector glanced at the page. 'At today's prices, the jewels are worth just over four lakhs of rupees.'

'Ade appa!' exclaimed Ayyadurai in awe.

'One of the pendants alone is worth half a lakh,' added the clerk, fingering his belt with an important air. His manner indicated that he considered himself to be the ultimate authority for everything in that office.

'Will this gentleman be entitled to any reward?' asked the collector, indicating Kalyanaraman.

'This ayya has put the record in writing and deposited the jewels in the treasury. So, yes, he is entitled to a reward.'

'How much?'

'That I cannot say till I consult the rules.'

'Please consult the rules right away.'

The clerk hitched up his belt and strode towards a cupboard. He pulled out a musty green book and put on his bifocal spectacles. Riffling through the pages, he paused at a particular page and started reading. 'In the matter of hidden treasure found, the Act of 1878 as read alongside the recommendations of the Board Resolution number 358 of March 24, 1950 …'

'Hold it!' interrupted Kalyanaraman. 'I don't want any part of the value of this treasure. The jewels belonged to Ratnavathy and they should be disposed of only according to her written wishes.'

'If the jewels actually belonged to Ratnavathy, they will all have to be handed over to the zamin's family by law,' remarked the clerk. 'They can't be called "hidden treasure" because the ownership is known in this case.'

Kalyanaraman pointed out, 'But Ratnavathy has written clearly in her diary that the jewels should under no circumstances go to anyone in the family, and that they should be used only for charitable purposes.'

The collector sought the opinion of his clerk. 'What do you say to that?'

'How can a diary be assumed to be a will? If the zamin's family takes the matter to the magistrate's court, there will be a huge problem.'

Kalyanaraman looked at the collector pleadingly.

The latter came up with a solution. 'Look, that very same diary is the only source that mentions the existence of the jewels. Kalyanaraman, you hold on to that diary. If anyone brings up the subject, I will merely say, "Diary? What diary? I don't know anything about it. I've never seen it." Then it is unclaimed treasure and becomes the property of the local government. We can use the amount to build a girls' high school and a public library right here in Mempatti.'

'Yes, and perhaps we can improve the bus stand also?' suggested the clerk.

'Bus stand? First of all there is no proper road to bring a bus to Mempatti,' Ayyadurai pointed out.

'I meant the bus stand in Mempalam,' said the smug clerk. 'Isn't that where everyone gets off to get to your village?'

'All right, I will get permission for two or three projects and get them built in Ratnavathy's name. What do you say, Mr Kalyanaraman?'

'I'm all for it, sir. That would be good.'

'Will you sign here to show you have agreed to this?'

Kalyanaraman signed the document.

'Tell me again, Husain, how did you nab the culprit?'

Superintendent Husain gave the collector a brief recap of the recent events.

'Kalyanaraman here was the one mainly responsible for the capture. He helped us a lot. The circumstances were not clear earlier, and so the inspector became thoroughly confused.' (Here the superintendent smiled meaningfully.)

'Who did you say the fellow is?'

'His name was Saminathan. The *peria* zamindar had mistresses in every town. This fellow Saminathan, alias Pazhaniandi, is his son by one of them. He grew up in Madras. He worked as a stage lighting artist and later as the bass player in a film orchestra. He went from job to job, even working as the driver of a tourist bus for some time.'

'And finally he landed up here? How did that happen?'

'His mother was a stage artiste and a contemporary of Tamil film stars such as V.A. Chellappa and T.P. Rajalakshmi. Mohanarangam was her name ... the fellow showed me a photo of her. He claimed that his mother knew all about Ratnavathy's jewels, because the zamindar had described the jewels and promised that he would gift them to her. She is the one who guessed that Ratnavathy had hidden the jewels. She told her son, "Those jewels are still in the zamindar's house; they have not gone anywhere. In bitterness and frustration, Ratnavathy would have buried or hidden them away somewhere before committing suicide." She had been urging her son to go to the zamindar's house and hunt for the treasure.

'For about six months he has been loitering around the village under the pretence of entertaining people with his bioscope at temple festivals. He hunted around the zamindar's house and surrounding areas ...'

‘And that woman Snehalatha? What about her?’ asked the collector.

‘That fellow’s accomplice,’ explained the superintendent. She is a case of someone who quit a convent school education to enter the film world only to be totally disillusioned. A daring woman ready to take risks. He had taken her on as a partner in his scheme. According to the plot they hatched in Madras, he was to come ahead and try to find the hidden treasure. If he failed she was to follow, pretending to be the zamindar’s granddaughter. Sir, that’s why, when his own efforts failed he wrote asking her to come.’

‘What do you think, Mr Kalyanaraman?’

‘In the letter he had written the sender’s town as “Chonnai” instead of “Chennai”. I was confused by that.’

‘It was probably done on purpose to confuse anyone who came across the letter by chance.’

‘If I’d reached the house about half an hour earlier I could have prevented the crime,’ said Kalyanaraman regretfully.

‘I doubt whether he had ever planned to kill her, Kalyanaraman. In a way it was her greed that brought her to this dreadful end.’

‘But she was a very clever woman, sir. She was able to understand the clue in the diary. She was shrewd enough to realize that Ratnavathy must have dropped the jewel box into the well.’

Ayyadurai agreed. ‘Yes, she was clever. With Marudamuthu’s help she got hold of a rope and a grappling iron and dredged the well to find the box. She must have half-immersed herself in the water to locate the box. What a tigress!’

‘But how is it that Marudamuthu didn’t see the contents of the box that he helped to raise from the well?’ the collector wanted to know.

‘She would have told him it contains some family items of sentimental value. Even if she had opened the box and shown him the contents, he would not have reacted. His thoughts would have been firmly fixed on the reward she had promised him in return for his help,' explained Kalyanaraman.

'Oh, I see!' said the collector, his face reddening slightly. 'And did she give him the reward?'

'Of course! How could she not?' said Kalyanaraman. 'It happened the following night when they both slipped away during the villu paatu. Velli came there later and found them together and was outraged … but that's another story …' Kalyanaraman shook his head as though to shake off unpleasant memories.

'So Marudamuthu's only involvement was in retrieving the box from the well?' asked the collector.

'Yes, that's all.'

'And the box was taken out the night before the murder took place?'

The superintendent took up the tale once more. 'Yes, and Saminathan alias Pazhaniandi the Bioscope Man was a witness to the happenings at the well. He watched as Marudamuthu went into the well and came out with a dripping wet box which he handed to Snehalatha. He saw them carry the box back to the house. He waited the whole of the next day thinking she would contact him and tell him, "Look, I've found the jewel box." But was she going to do that? Of course not! The sight of that mound of precious jewels roused her greed. Why share it with her partner? So she pretended nothing had happened.

'The following night, after the temple festival celebrations were over, Bioscope Man went to meet Snehalatha at the zamin house. By that time, Marudamuthu had come, received his "reward" and left. Velli had come, poured out her heart, shouted abuses and gone home, miserable.

'Bioscope Man confronts Snehalatha. There is no sign of the box in her room. "Where's the box that you and Marudamuthu drew out of the well last night? Where have you hidden it?" he asks. "What box? I don't know about any box. If you know so much, why don't you go and find it?" she challenges him. He searches every corner of the room. No box. He threatens her. "Tell me where you've hidden it, or else ..." "I swear I don't know what you're talking about!" she says.

'At that point, the fellow flies into a fury. Though he is fifty-plus in age, he is still strong and muscular. He twists her arms, half-throttles her, till she is forced to reveal the hiding place of the box ... in a crevice, on a ledge, inside the well. Having got his answer, he throws her aside roughly. She falls awkwardly, hitting the back of her head hard on the wall. She slumps down to the floor in the room, half-sitting against the wall. She is dead.

'Velli arrives. Bioscope Man hides. It is dark in the room. Velli abuses Snehalatha, leaves the doll and the vibhuti, throws a small stone at the dead Snehalatha and goes away.

'Bioscope Man has not planned to kill Snehalatha. So now he has no plan to get rid of her body. He decides it is best to throw her body into the well. He starts dragging her towards the well. But before he can complete his plan he hears approaching footsteps and runs away.

'That is when Kalyanaraman arrives and tracks the bloodstains, finds the body ...'

'Yes,' put in Kalyanaraman, 'and then the case takes a twist and Velli becomes a suspect. When the rumour was deliberately spread that she has been arrested for the murder and that the police have locked up the house and gone away, Bioscope Man decides to come back to the well and get the box ... and gets nabbed red-handed!'

'Very strange, the whole thing,' remarked the collector.

'Family jewels that carried a curse! They took the lives of three generations of the family,' remarked the superintendent.

Ayyadurai added, 'It's said that Ratnavathy's great-great-grandfather bought a lot of land and houses, cheating people right and left. He is thought to have made many enemies even then. These jewels were acquired by him out of ill-gotten wealth.'

The clerk placed a sheet of paper on the table before the collector. The latter glanced at it. 'The assessor has come. Kalyanaraman, are you sure you don't want to claim any share in the jewels?'

'Yes, I'm absolutely sure.'

'You'll be staying in the village a while, I hope?'

'I'll leave for Madras in a week.'

'Oh, so your folk music research is over?'

'No, no, it has barely begun! I was able to collect quite a lot of songs here, and there may be more. But the memories are driving me away ... that house, Snehalatha, Velli, all the happenings ... maybe I'll return after some time. But I doubt I will ever forget that house!'

'In any case Mister Kalyanaraman has to come back for the trial and appear as a witness,' reminded the inspector.

'I know,' said Kalyanaraman. 'Sir, I'll take leave of you now.'

'Best of luck!'

Kalyanaraman shook hands with the collector and left.

Train no. 301 had not yet arrived at Thirunilam station. A blue suitcase stood on the platform, and Kalyanaraman stood near it wearing dark glasses and a camera around his neck.

Ayyadurai was not present because of some religious impediment to his being there. But a largish group was there to see Kalyanaraman off. Thangarasu was there, and Periatha too. Marudamuthu had come, as had Velli's father and Velli herself.

'We are all very happy that you came and stayed in our village,' said Thangarasu. Everything was going so well, but somewhere in between some unfortunate things happened ... all caused by women, did you notice? What do you say, Periatha?'

'My prince! Can't you take me with you? After you go away who will give me money for betel leaves, a measure of rice and some malli coffee? My son's second wife ... because she's pregnant I slave and grind cotton to earn a few coins to bring home for her, but the wretched creature ... *pandiar kuthirai thandutham kadal* ... the way she carries on ...!'

'Keep quiet, old woman! Ayya isn't interested in your family problems.'

'That Snehalatha ... she was the spitting image of Ratnavathy.'

'Pah! Old hag!'

'What do you say, Marudamuthu?' asked Periatha.

'You and your stupid tongue!' was his retort. Turning towards Kalyanaraman he said, 'Ayya, I behaved badly at the hearing. In the presence of the public I spoke disrespectfully to my elders. I fell under the spell of that witch and almost lost my precious jewel, my Velli. My good sense is now restored. Mama, tell him,' he urged Velli's father who was standing by.

'We just have to put all that's happened behind us. Just forget the whole thing as if it was a bad dream. Can a recent attraction replace a years-old relationship? I knew all along how this would turn out. Young blood can cause a fling now and then. But good sense will prevail in the end. When we men see an attractive woman, we feel a surge of desire; that's how we men are made. But can long-term relationships and promises be broken for such passing feelings? No! And they will never be allowed to be broken!'

Velli stood silently staring down at the ground. The dark goddess who had burnished her beautiful image and chosen to imprison herself in a special aperture within Kalyanaraman's heart.

'Are you happy now, Velli?'

Silence.

'You are going to get the husband you were longing for. So you're happy, aren't you?'

Silence.

'She is shy, saar.'

'Velli, will you stop selling cucumbers at the station?'

She shook her head without lifting her gaze from the ground.

'Shall I take a photo of you?'

Again a shake of the head. No.

'Will you remember me, Velli?'

'How can she forget you?' cut in Thangarasu.

'Hold on, let her answer,' said Kalyanaraman.

She nodded yes.

'Won't you speak?'

Silence.

'Ey, pilla, why don't you answer? Ayya is talking to you.'

'What's that scar on your arm?' asked someone in the group.

'That's where a girl scratched me with her sharp nails.'

Velli quickly lifted her head and looked at Kalyanaraman's arm. She lifted her gaze to his face. Her eyes were moist with tears. As he watched her, more tears welled up and her lips twitched. She was trying to convey something. There was something different about her ... something ...

Dang! Dang! Dang! The blue-shirted railway clerk struck energetically several times on the piece of railing that hung from a tree and served as a bell. After a slight pause, he struck it three more times for emphasis.

An imaginary dialogue ran through Kalyanaraman's mind.

'Velli, what's on your mind? What were you trying to convey to me?'

'Ayya, I didn't realize earlier that you are fond of me. Just say the word and I will leave everything and come with you right now.'

'Velli, I lack the courage to do that. You too are not brave enough to take that leap. How I wish I could be like Prithviraj and carry you away on my horse ...'

Thakadak ... thakadak ... thakadak. He rode up on a tall Arabian steed, scooped up Velli with one arm circling her waist, seated her in front of him and rode away ...

Train no. 301 pulled into Thirunilam station in its usual reluctant way.

'Ayya, the next time you visit here, you will see Velli with a baby in her arms,' said Marudamuthu. 'What are you eating, Rajavelu? Is it *kamarkattu*?'

Kalyanaraman climbed into a First Class compartment. Marudamuthu brought the suitcase and neatened Kalyanaraman's berth. 'Look, Velli!' called Marudamuthu.

Velli turned. CLICK!

A photograph as a final memory.

'Akka, ask him to take a photo of me too, please, please!' begged Rajavelu.

The guard blew his whistle.

'Marudamuthu, get off the train!' called voices from the platform. Marudamuthu jumped out.

The train pulled out from the platform belching a puff of steam as it set off.

Not yet too late to snatch her, put her in the suitcase, take her ...

'Goodbye, Thangarasu, Marudamuthu, Periatha, Rajavelu ... Velli ...'

I could pull the chain to stop the train ...

The train picked up speed. Velli's figure grew smaller and smaller ...

Kalyanaraman watched her till she disappeared in the distance.

What had she been trying to tell him?

What was on her mind? What was in her heart?

As advised by men of yore
I have completed this tale.
All those who read it wisely
And those who recount it by word of mouth,
May they all prosper!

Translator's Note

WHAT A JOY IT is to translate Sujatha! Not that it is an easy task. Indeed it is a challenge, but one that is energizing and stimulating.

Having translated some short stories of his earlier, I approached this work with a great deal of eager anticipation. Sure enough, it is replete with his hallmark touches of character insights, humour, irony and a wholesome appreciation for the absurdities of life.

As a translator, instead of reading the whole novel before I get started with translating it, I have always preferred to read and tell the story as I go along, imparting the freshness of first impressions. This approach is especially helpful in serialized stories like this one. What does the next chapter have in store? I wait to find out, like any reader of the book. Here I found myself often chuckling aloud as I typed, enjoying the way the story was unfolding, in a different language but hopefully with its tone and DNA intact.

Sujatha is an author who has always defied stereotypes. His works span several genres and even time zones. Is this novel a romance? A social drama? A mystery? A psychological exploration of characters? The short answer – it is all these with a good dose of humour mixed in.

Set in a typical Tamil Nadu village but featuring a far-from-typical 'haunted' mansion, there are memorable montages aplenty: the *paatu* at the village festival; the ghost that moans in the tamarind tree; the diary with its hint of hidden treasure;

a chicken running around with its head cut off; and many more. I found myself having to refine my first drafts of many of these cameos to convey to the reader, as best I could, the images they conjured up in my mind.

The novel is well-paced and cleverly crafted. All the characters live and breathe and are totally relatable: the young folk music researcher from Madras; an unexpected visitor who may not be what she seems; the charming village belle; the casters of spells, both romantic and occult; villagers old and young, naive and crafty – a mosaic of personalities.

The denouement is a twist in the tale. That is enough of a spoiler alert!

I am grateful to the Tamil Nadu Textbook and Educational Services Corporation (TNTB) for giving me the opportunity to translate this outstanding novel.

About the Author

'Sujatha' (1935–2008) was the pseudonym adopted by the prolific and extremely popular Tamil writer S. Rangarajan, who wrote several short stories, plays, poems and articles in addition to many novels. His subjects ranged from domestic dramas to mysteries, romances and popular science.

An engineer by qualification, Sujatha was instrumental in designing the electronic voting machine. He also collaborated on scripts for films with Kamal Hassan (*Vikram*), Mani Ratnam (*Thiruda Thiruda*) and others.

About the Translator

Malini Seshadri is a writer, editor and translator. Her translations from Tamil to English include *Vanmam* and *Just One Word* by Bama, as well as contributions to short story anthologies.